I0646276

RICK KUEBER

THE GENESIS PROJECT

The Convergence Saga
Book 2

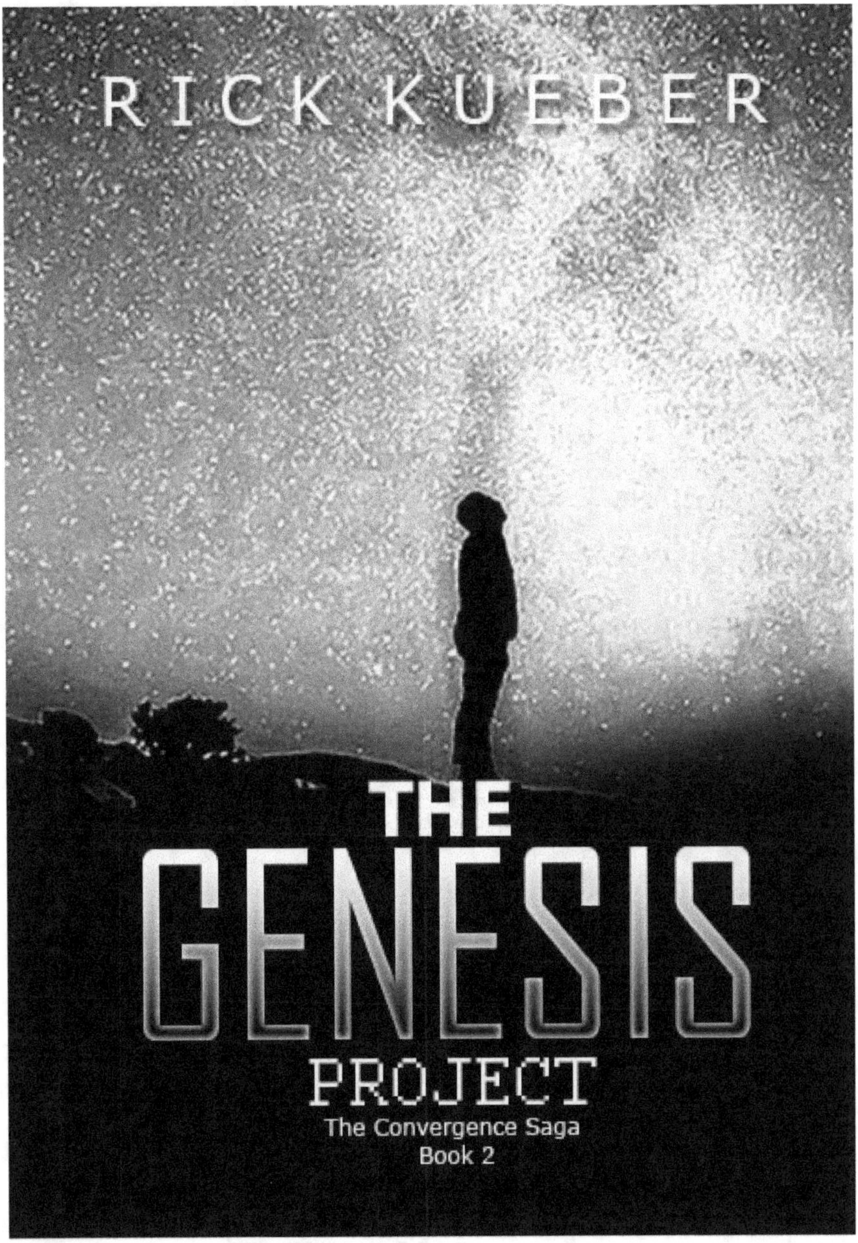

The Genesis Project

Cover Art Design by Annette Munnich

Copyright © 2016
ISBN 978-0692688953
Stellium Books
www.stelliumbooks.com
Grant Park Illinois 60940

The Genesis Project

The Convergence Saga

Book 2

by

Rick Kueber

Dedication

As always this book is dedicated to my son Daniel,

Also to Annette for all of her hard work and dedication and Tabitha whose creative soul inspired me to create something unique and beautiful.

Table Of Contents

The Genesis Project

Chapter 1

The Road Less Traveled

The seemingly mindless chanting of the Takers echoed in my head and throughout the forest, hauntingly. Standing at the precipice of the ravine, the brilliant ball of fire, we call the sun, was past midday. I had lost track of time. It seemed like only a few hours since I had slipped on board the Titan, but the more I thought about all of the information in my head and everything that had happened, everything that had changed... it could have been days or even weeks. Each physical encounter with an Ahsusha, or alien being, had resulted in a loss of memory and a period of complete confusion. With no one and nothing to relate time to, I was lost.

I was not only lost in time, I was physically lost. How far we had traveled in the Titan was a mystery and I could only hope that I could find Barnhill again. I did not know if Elle would be there if Maddie would be there and be okay, or even alive, but... it was the last place I knew they had been. I had to find my way back there, if for no other reason, to begin my search for them. The decision to retrace the path of the Titan was my best bet to find the town, but it was sort of a shot in the dark. The Titan could have wandered for days, zigzagging across the wilderness. Barnhill could be less than a few miles away as the crow flies, but the Titan's path might have traveled dozens or even hundreds of miles. I began to feel overwhelmed and uncertain of my path. The one thing that I was certain of... I was starving.

I left the chanting hoard behind me and followed what appeared to be the path of the Titan. I searched the sparse forest for anything that seemed edible. There were no berry bushes, no nut trees that I could find and I thought about the odds of trapping a hare, of finding a lizard or turtle... I had no way to start a fire. Depression began to set in. A drink of lemonade and one of those dry cereal bars... I would kill for a bite of one of Elle's dry cereal bars. Pains in my stomach poked at me like dull knives tearing at my insides. Nearly a full day of walking had left me no closer to finding any sustenance and my anxiety and psychological state had left me feeling that I may be no closer to finding my one true friend.

As the tormenting sun began to sink lower in the sky on my second day of walking, dying from starvation seemed more likely than ever finding my way back. Sitting on a hard slab of sandstone, with my head in my hands, the voices in my head argued. A weak and timid persona swayed me to believe that giving up,, curling up, and waiting to die was inevitable. Another more commanding voice told me to fill my stomach with anything, even dirt, and grasses, to ease the pain, but to never give up because I had a greater purpose... I would have never made it this far if I did not. A twisted conifer wrapped itself around me like it was hugging me, or shielding me though its spindly form was far from comforting or protective. My body, weak and exhausted, crumpled over on the hard slab and I drifted off to a delirious slumber.

Several hours of uninterrupted sleep had passed when I heard a familiar voice.

"Hey you... Wake up... you need to eat something." The voice of Elle filled my head with comfort. How she managed to find me in the middle of the wilderness, I had no idea, but I knew she was right.

"Elle..." I groaned sleepily, trying to clear my blurry, waking vision.

"Eat something... anything... baby." Her hand reached out to me and she ran her fingers through my hair and leaned in, sniffing my cheek... and then licking it.

I awoke with a start from a dream that I wished, more than anything, had been real. The stars filled the night sky and the sliver of a moon smiled down on my desperate situation. 'Sniff-sniff'. I flinched and my head spun to the side. There, laying nuzzled up beside me was a full grown golden retriever... not an old dog, but no pup either.

"Where did you come from?" I asked out loud as if this canine would somehow answer me back. He did answer in his own way. He sat up and his tail wagged vigorously.

A smile broke across my face, despite the wrenching cramps in my empty gut. Leaning on one hand, I rubbed his head with my free hand, scratching his yellow fur and floppy ears. He seemed quite content to have found a companion. While I petted and stroked his coat, I began to notice movement nearby. This was not the movement of wandering Takers, or even a random deer or coyote. What I was noticing was a flurry of insects scavenging around on the forest floor. Elle's words haunted my thoughts... *'Eat something... anything'*. A primal instinct took over and I began to gasp at the tiny movements and quickly began shoving crickets, beetles and anything I could grab, into my mouth, crunching and squishing their disgusting shells and guts as if they were delicacies as if my life depended on it... which it did.

When I could no longer force myself to devour any more of the foul bugs, I peeled a small patch of moss from the base of the twisted cedar and began to chew on it to clear my mouth of the repulsive taste and feel of the insect bits and pieces that remained lodged, with nothing to wash it all down with. Much to my surprise and pleasure, the moss held a considerable amount of moisture and also caused my mouth to water. The retriever sat and eagerly watched as I fed myself on insects and the clumps of moss.

I reached up and rubbed his neck, feeling for a collar. A wide, nylon, green and blue, weaved collar had been buried and hidden beneath his thick and matted coat. Both hands took hold of it and my fingers searched the collar. A jingling sound was like music to my ears. It is quite amazing how much the smallest of things can bring a smile and satisfaction when you have nothing. The jingle came from two dog tags that dangled from the well-worn collar and I slipped the collar to the side, in order to get a better look at the tags. The first was an official silver tag and let me know that the pooch had been well cared for and was up to date on his shots. The second was a metallic yellow-colored tag and held the information I had hoped for. His home was on Joshua Lane in Barnhill, his name was Josie, and *'he'* was a she. The best news was the name of the town, Barnhill. Dogs have been known to wander from one side of the country to the other, but perhaps Josie would lead me back to her home.

I was feeling a bit rested, and although a bit queasy, my hunger pangs were tolerable. It was hours before sunrise, but I was no longer concerned about running into any Takers or Titans. I stood up and Josie perked up, jumping up on me, bouncing on her back feet excitedly. I ruffled her ears and head in my hands and put my nose right up to her cold and wet nose.

"Hey, Josie girl!" I spoke to her as if I were speaking to a very young child or a dog of my own, in an energy-filled voice that wasn't really mine. "You wanna go home? Come on girl, let's go home."

Josie jumped up and licked me square on the mouth, and her butt wiggled and her tail wagged in a most feverish way. Though I had no idea of the exact direction, I took a couple of steps to the east, in the same direction I had been traveling the day before. Josie trotted ahead a few paces, but then stopped abruptly and turned to see if I was following behind. When I caught up to her, I patted her side and stroked her coat. Josie panted and looked straight into my glowing eyes without fear or question. This dog had befriended a total stranger, simply on the basis that I was willing to be kind to her and be her friend too.

The remainder of the night, and most of the next day continued in much the same way: Josie running ahead and then waiting for me to catch up. She instinctively knew where the best and safest paths were and it felt, to me, as if we were headed in the right direction. Without warning, after catching up to Josie just an hour or so before the sun began to set on our first day together, she nuzzled my hand with her head and nose and took off to our right, in a ninety-degree angle from the direction we had been heading. I wondered if she had been distracted by a small animal or scent, and I began to worry that maybe she was just wandering through the forest in no particular direction.

She darted out of my sight but soon came rushing back. Josie circled me twice, and jumping up, pawed at me... whimpering to get my attention.

"Get down girl..." I said in my doggie-talk voice. "You're gonna get me all muddy." A sudden wave of excitement poured over me and hope tingled throughout my body. Josie's paws were muddy, and muddy paws meant... water! "Let's go Josie girl! Let's go!" Somehow I found a surge of hidden energy and I nearly ran after her, through a briar thicket and up a small hill. On my descent down the other side, I watched and literally teared up when I saw Josie galloping down the hill and then leap into a small stream that ran between two spoil-bank hills. She splashed and frolicked in the shallow water and I felt as if I could splash right along with her... I felt as if she may have just saved my life.

I bolted down the hill faster than my feet could carry me. Two-thirds of the way down, my momentum overtook my coordination. I tumbled forward with my feet flying up behind me, my right shoulder and the side of my face planting and then dragging through the leaves and sticks that covered the forest floor. I completed my tumble with my back pounding hard against the hillside, knocking the wind out of me as I slid down the remainder of the hill. Twigs and exposed roots scraped my shoulders, neck, and back, and the back of my skull and my ear were scratched and bleeding when I came to rest at the bottom, against a young sapling. Pain and anger washed over me but quickly vanished when Josie trotted up, licking my face, whimpering, and dripping creek-water on me. I quickly recovered my composure and though I was cut up, bruised and sore, I managed to regain my footing, sauntered over to the stream and knelt down over it. I dipped my hands in the cool running water and raised them to my face as if saying a prayer and giving thanks to mother earth.

I cupped my hands and scooped up the crystal clear water, drinking up as much as I could contain. The cool water trickled between my tightly closed fingers, spattering the creek like raindrops and running down my forearms to my elbows. I had been given hope from man's best friend. This was the second time since the appearance of the Titans that I had been saved by a female... first Elle, and now Josie. Elle... a picture of her face, and the feeling of holding her intimately close, was burned into my memory.

Alien invaders, zombie-like Takers, hybrid Ahsushas, and my own strange adaptation and mixture of alien traits... not to mention this feeling that I was an intentional pivot point of some type of revolution... and yet for some reason, Elle was the thing that filled my thoughts. She had become not only the most important thing in my world... in only a few short weeks, she had become my world.

After filling my belly with cool stream water, and watching Josie playing so contently, I pulled my long sleeved t-shirt (that used to be white) over my head and kicked off my shoes. Unbuttoning and unzipping the blue jeans that Elle had found for me, I shimmied them off. The stream was only a couple of feet wide and less than a foot deep, but it was the closest thing to a bath I had and the cool running water was exhilarating as it rushed over my parched and overheated skin. I knelt in the creek, naked and exposed for all of nature to see, and rinsed my clothes in its swift flowing beauty. I sat in the water, splashing myself and soaking up the life-giving element.

Standing up, I began to awkwardly don my sopping wet clothes. The jeans seemed to weigh a ton and even though they were uncomfortably soaked, I knew they would probably dry out all too quickly. I pulled the long-sleeved, cotton t-shirt back over my head, and the neck stretched out unnaturally. Putting the jeans on was difficult, but the dripping wet shirt was nearly impossible. It clung to me like sticky-tape and I felt like a child who was learning to dress himself for the first time. When I finally had it on, it hung loosely and seemed over-sized, which made me feel even more childlike. Josie played and splashed downstream and lapped up as much water as she could hold. After over an hour of fluid bliss, I slipped on my shoes and called out to my new traveling companion.

"Come on girl, let's go home," I said, thinking if I said a simple and possibly familiar phrase, she might understand in the way dogs understand basic verbal commands. I had no doubt that dogs, and many animals, understood emotions and physical cues. Josie jumped into action with my words and that gave me hope that she recognized something I had said, and I had hopes that if there was only one word that she was reacting to, that word was *home*.

We trekked along as the sunset turned the sky from an unremarkable pale blue palette, dotted with puffy cotton balls, to a canvas covered in a dozen shades of oranges, reds, and purples as if Monet himself had painted it with blurry watercolors, that began to show more and more through the treetops as the forest thinned out. I tried to keep the thin ribbon of the stream in my view as long as I could, but after a few hours of the night, we had drifted too far left of where it had trickled through the almost mountainous woods.

The days in the desert had been searing, and in this forest, they had been smotheringly sultry, but the night was quickly growing cool, and my clothes were still slightly on the damp side. I longed for a fire, and a bed and blanket... and Elle. While we journeyed, I searched for a resting spot, but no real shelter could be found. When the sky had darkened and pinpoints of starlight speckled the evening sky, we began to pass through a grove of evergreens. This patch of pines was more dense than the sparse woods we had been wandering through and the thick layer of dead pine needles felt soft underfoot. I chose this spot to spend the night and Josie quickly agreed. Nearly laying on the ground, I used the entire length of my arms and hands to scoop the thick layer of needles into a large pile, a few feet wide, over six feet in length and nearly eight inches thick. Though it took quite some time, I didn't mind; I had nothing else to do. Josie sat nearby, watching intently and I worked. When I had finished, I glanced over at her and her big dark eyes had the most pitiful look. I felt a little guilty, so I started scooping up more needled together to make another spot for her. I made her bedding in a circular shape, about three foot across and almost as thick as what I had made for myself. When I was finished, I looked over and saw her sitting with her mouth open, tongue hanging out, appearing to smile if that were a possibility... I had been played by a retriever.

"There you go girl." I gently whispered as I patted the palette of pine needles. Josie stood up, slowly stepped up onto her bed and after turning three full circles, laid down. Tucking her nose under her tail, she turned into a dirty yellow furball. I sat down next to her and petted her soft coat, and let myself unwind for a few minutes before lying down. A flurry of thoughts spun recklessly in my head as I sat quietly: pictures of Elle and I carelessly goofing around, little Maddie's quest for a peanut-butter sandwich, a mental and physical connection with the Titan, the chanting of the Takers, a night of confusion and awakening in a vast desert, the death of Bobby...

When the thoughts slowed and my mind's worry eased, I worked my way into my own pile of pines, laid down, and thought of days gone by and futures that might have been as I slipped away to a peaceful dreamland...

It was a crisp and early morning, just before sunrise. I wandered down an empty street in a large, deserted city. The view was as cold and empty as the winter air that nipped at my nose and stung my ears. The chill was the only thing that even touched my senses. The silence was deafening and not even the sound of wind could be heard. There was no smell of car exhaust or breakfast cooking at a sidewalk bistro. It seemed a dead and barren, urban wasteland. Turning the gray, concrete corner my footsteps stopped abruptly. Towering over the city, a blackish-blue Titan seemed to stare down at me. Anxiety filled my stomach with knots and butterflies, and as I watched the Titan fade from the darkest blue imaginable to a pale chalky white, the sound of church bells rang out from a different direction than the Titan.

Like a lab rat in a maze, searching for the chunk of cheddar at the finish line, I took off in search of the bells. Running down the streets, turning corners in hopes of finding the source before the melodic ringing ended, I felt like I was trapped in some lost episode of The Twilight Zone. A cold sweat beaded on my forehead and dampened my upper lip. I zipped around the corner of an older brick building. The echoing shock of the last ringing of the bells, and the sight of a Gothic-looking, limestone cathedral filled me with awe. Its steeple, crowned with a copper cross, tarnished and green from exposure, towered over the skyline. I slowed to a cautious walk when I climbed the weather-stained steps. A set of immense, ornate wooden doors lay before me and swung open effortlessly before I could even reach for them.

I stepped through the entryway like I was stepping through some mystical portal. Breezing through the vestibule and into the sanctuary, I found pews filled with people of all shapes, sizes, ages... every race, creed, and color... A long line had formed up the center aisle as if waiting their turn for 'Holy Communion'. I turned my gaze to where the pastor or priest should be, but instead, there was a man in everyday, street clothes, bent over to the young woman in front of him. His face was hidden from my view by the full, jet black hair of the woman at the front of the line. When she had finished, she turned to return down the aisle. The blood ran from my face and I felt faint when I saw her glowing eyes.

"ELLE!" I cried out in disbelief.

Everyone in the congregation and the line turned to look at me. My knees went weak and I trembled all over when I watched the sea of glowing eyes land their stares directly on me, with their arms outstretched. The man at the head of the line, where the pastor should have been stood up straight and tall, dropping the chalice from his hand and blood poured from it, splattering and spilling out on the floor beneath it. His dazed look was only surpassed by my own when I looked into his glowing eyes and met my own reflection, my face... it was me. The scene went blood red and then black.

The dream ended, but I managed to sleep a while longer until a wriggling stirred me. More than half asleep, I rolled onto my side and wrapped my arm around Josie. I buried my frosty face in the back of her neck and soaked up her warmth for another hour, trying to wake up, trying to remember and process the frighteningly, realistic dream.

Chapter 2

Unexpected

There was nothing I wanted more than to go back to the life that I once had, long before the appearance of the Titans, even though I really had only one confusing and terrifying memory of it. My body ached and felt like it should have popped and crackled like twisting bubble wrap when I stood up and stretched. The morning was cooler than I had been used to, and even though the pine needle bed did insulate me from the unforgiving, cold hard ground, it was no pillow-top mattress. Josie jumped to attention, excitedly, and stood by my side with her tail wagging wildly.

"Good morning Josie-girl," I smiled at her, glad to have a traveling companion. "What do you say we get ourselves home?"

As if she understood, or read my mind, Josie took off, trotting ahead and then waiting for me to catch up, like the day before. We walked for hours without stopping, or resting, and Josie led us out of the woods and across a wide open and mostly flat field of tall grasses that reached out to the horizon and beyond. We wandered lazily through the knee high weeds and grasses, not because we had no purpose, but because we had no food or water and even Josie's energy was obviously fading. The tree line began to shrink behind us and as the edge of a new woods appeared in the distance and to our right, a gathering of clouds began to build overhead. They weren't threatening clouds, but heavy, gray clouds that took the warmth away from the day.

With every step, the distant trees grew taller and more concerning. I had no doubt that someone or something was watching us from within the woods. Adrenaline rushed through my veins like the cool breeze that whispered through the waving green grasses, instantly clearing my sinuses and heightening my senses. This feeling wasn't telling me that it was an alien or Ashusha observing me, but it also didn't feel like it was a friend, like Elle. My steps became more intentional and my eyes constantly swept the woods, unsure if we should continue on our current heading, or shift left and away from the woods. I patted my thigh three times quickly, to call Josie to my side. She obediently returned to me and stuck by me as we walked on. There was comfort in trusting her instincts and she showed no signs of concern, so together, we continued on. Time seemed to pass more swiftly than the distance before us. The hidden sun crossed the clouded sky at a pace that exceeded our crossing of the expansive field, but eventually, the edge of the woods grew close enough that it almost seemed to close in around us.

Josie and I froze in our tracks when a whistling sound came from the trees to our right. Without warning, Josie took off running for the tree line and I hesitated, unsure if I should follow and chase after her, wait to see what would happen, or run in the opposite direction. She had saved me by leading me to water and had befriended me without question... I was beholden and gave chase. I could be running directly into a trap, right into resistance, or another encounter with unfriendly gunfire. None of that mattered at the moment. I couldn't leave Josie, and I had to make sure she was safe. Once again, only louder and more discernible than before, the whistling sound broke the near silence that surrounded me, and for the first time, I heard Josie bark... more of a 'woof' really.

"Just hold it right there if you don't want any trouble." A gruff voice said as a rather large man, dressed in camouflage hunting clothes, and 'camo' face paint, stepped out from behind a tree. "Stop right there, I said!" He did not shout, but his voice was stern and demanding... not to mention, he had a rifle pointed directly at me. I stopped dead in my tracks and slowly raised my hands to show my willing 'surrender'.

"Who are you and where'd you find Josie?" His voice sounded angered, but also confused as he put his cheek to the rifle and held me in his sights.

"My name is Tanner, and I was lost in the wilderness when 'Josie' found me. I've been walking with her and following her lead for a few days. I had hoped she would lead me someplace I could find some food and water." I chose not to say anything about my past, including my search for Elle and Maddie. I didn't know anything about this man, including whether or not I could trust him.

"Well Mr. Tanner, can you give me one good reason why I shouldn't shoot a glowing-eyed, alien-dude, right now?" The tension and nervousness showed in the fluctuating tone of his voice.

"I'm not an alien dude..." I stumbled over my words, unsure of how to explain my peculiar situation. "I was attacked by one of those alien things, but when it tried to take me over, it died, I guess... but it did make my eyes glow. I don't know what else I can say, other than I don't want to hurt anyone, except for more aliens." I was being honest though I withheld some of the story. "I have killed two of the alien things, and I even took down a Titan, one of those giant crafts, about three days walk... that way." I pointed in the direction we had come from.

"Well, that all sounds good and well, but I've never talked to one of you alien people, so I don't know... no reason why you wouldn't be lying." Though his words were filled with distrust, he lowered the barrel of the rifle and the intense look on his face eased. "This way..." He motioned with the barrel of the gun. "Come on Josie."

The golden retriever took to my side and nuzzled my hand, begging for attention and to be petted. The gun toting, camouflage-covered stranger noticed her acceptance of me. We walked along silently through the woods for a while, and even though he seemed to be less intimidated and leery of my intentions, the stranger kept a constant eye on me and through body language and non-verbal direction, kept me one step ahead of him.

"Just another mile or so, up that way." He actually pointed with his gloved hand, up a sharp, tree covered hill to our left. "By the way, I'm Kevin."

"Nice to meet you, Kevin," I said, honestly glad to have found another human being who may lead me to food, water and a comfortable place to sleep. "I wish we had met under better circumstances, though."

There was an awkward pause as if he was unsure of how to react. "I can't say I wish we had met under any circumstances, but I know what you mean."

We trekked arduously up the steep hill. I could hear Kevin's labored breathing as we fought against gravity to reach the peak. Josie, on the other hand, sprinted to the top, where she sat looking down on us, and patiently waited. Finishing the climb minutes before Kevin, I took a seat on the crest of the hill next to Josie, where I caught my breath and relaxed for a minute. Kevin huffed as he struggled his way to the top and let out an exasperated sigh when he threw his arms back and collapsed on the ground next to Josie and me.

"Jesus, I'm out of shape!" He moaned out and I literally laughed out loud.

"Ever since my first encounter with one of those alien things, I did notice I have a little more stamina than I used to, but that was a hell of a climb," I said as I tussled Josie's head and ears.

After a bit of a rest, Kevin sat up and reaching inside of his hunter's jacket, withdrew a thin, khaki canteen. Unscrewing the cap, he took a full drink and audibly exhaled. Had I not been so dehydrated, my mouth would have surely watered. I wanted nothing more than to take the canteen from his hand and gulp it down, saving some for Josie, of course.   Though my intention was to remain strong and appear independent, I failed miserably as I stared longingly at the canteen. Reluctantly, he handed it to me.

"You aren't... *contagious*, are you?" He said before he let go of his canteen.

"No, I spent over a week sharing water and food with a few people and so far... no glowing eyes." I tried to make light of my condition, but he seemed put off by my remarks.

"So... where are these people now?" His words projected guilt and cynicism. "Save some for Josie."

"We got separated, and I'm trying to find my way back to them now. Where are we headed, if you don't mind me asking?" I said after taking a long needed drink of water. I turned my attention to Josie and carefully poured the water from the canteen to my hand while she lapped it up, placidly.

"I have a small hunting cabin just over the next hill." He turned his head, looking behind him; in the direction we were headed. "We can rest there and I have more water and a little food there. I'm guessing Josie and you are hungry?" He posed the statement as a question.

"Starving..." I mumbled, thinking of my last meal of moss and bugs.

"Well, if you're starving, she's probably starving too, and I've had her since she was a puppy..." I could see the gratitude in his eyes and knew he was truly thankful that she had returned to him.

We took to walking again, but Kevin seemed much more comfortable than before, and I felt less like he was a guard and I was a prisoner, and more like he was just a guy who had rescued a lost hiker. We talked a little, but mostly he talked to the retriever. I didn't mind. In fact, I was glad that he had been reunited with his dog and the fact that he showed her more attention than me, was reassuring.

"There it is." He said with fervor.

"Now *that*..." I began. "...is a sight for sore eyes!"

"Even glowing ones?" Kevin cynically joked, and then awkwardly tried to take the words back, but he could think of nothing to say that would change the harsh words.

"Yeah... even glowing ones," I smiled, to try to disperse the uncomfortable hostility between us.

The cabin was within our sights and for all intents and purposes, looked more like a shanty built by a homeless person who had scavenged bits and pieces of scraps from a condemned house. In all honesty, it looked like nothing more than a plain wood sided box with one window, a door, and a sloping, flat roof. The wooden exterior was weathered gray with some black, splotchy patches of mildew and a dying ivy of some sort that grew sparsely on the front left corner. All the same, it was shelter, and there was a promise of more water and even food. Approaching the cabin, the sky let loose of a light and chilling rain.

"What happened to the heat?" I asked my new trail guide as he reached for the rickety and poorly hung 'cabin' door.

"Uh... fall, I guess." He said with a tone of confusion. "It *is* September. It's always a roller-coaster of hot and cold in September around here." He shot me a curious look over his shoulder as he opened the door, allowing Josie to rush inside. "You aren't from around here are you... I mean..."

"Indiana, originally, I suppose..." I sensed the regret in his wording, unintentionally implying that I was '*alien*' and not just to these parts.

The interior of the cabin was dimly lit by the overcast daylight that snuck in through the dirty window and open door. I followed Kevin inside and though it darkened some when I closed the door behind me, the interior had a warm and cozy feel to it, unlike what I had expected. Kevin's back was turned and I could hear the sound of swift stroking of metal on metal. I was unsure of its true source until a cracking sound caught my attention. He had struck an old style, wooden kitchen match and soon had lit a kerosene lantern, filling the tiny cabin with a pale glow. Being well lit, I could now see that the walls were finished paneling, and they were probably insulated too. Two small cot-like beds lined two of the walls, an eight-quart cooler sat on a small table that was accompanied by two folding chairs. I was pleased with the small space I had been offered, but the one thing that caught my eye most was a small, free standing, wood burning stove. Whether or not Kevin had firewood, or would risk a fire, the thought of a crackling fire and maybe even some warm food sounded heavenly.

"This place is great." I thanked him for taking me in. "Do you mind if I lie down on one of your beds?"

"Go ahead." He said, pointing to one of the cots specifically. "I'm going to fire up the wood burner. You like fried ham steak?"

I almost felt faint at the thought of real food. "I love ham... but I don't remember the last time I had it. I'd be happy to eat it cold right now, but if you want to fry it, I won't argue one bit."

I sank into the wool blanket covered cot. I grabbed the small pillow from one end, curled up on my side and tucked it under my head. The sounds of Kevin clunking around, going in and out of the door and smoky smell of him stoking up a fire, filled my senses as I laid there with eyes closed, resting. The aromatic scent that escaped the old black iron stove made my thoughts drift to unfamiliar memories of sitting around a campfire with friends and building a fire in an ornate, brick fireplace at home with my family. Where those people were and what had become of them was a mystery to me... who those people were was just as much of an enigma. Part of me wanted to solve that mystery, but there was another piece of me that only wanted to find Elle, understand my perplexing role in this apocalyptic world, and move forward with my life.

A new sound and scent aroused me from my distant thoughts. There was a muffled clunking, followed by a sizzling sound and my nose was teased by the tempting aroma of frying, salted pork. I came to my senses quickly and sat up on the edge of the cot. I took in a deep breath through my nose and let out a sigh. I rubbed my eyes, ran my fingers through my hair, and across the slow growth of a beard on my face. I looked over to the stove, where Kevin sat in one of the folding chairs with his back to me, and noticed there was an aluminum sauce pan steaming away on the stove as well as the skillet that seared the heavenly ham.

"Dear god, that smells amazing!" I blurted out and slightly startled the chef.

"Oh... thanks." He said, genuinely accepting my accolade. "It's not much, but it's better than nothing."

He lifted the skillet from the stove, turned to the table, and pulled the two ham steaks from the pan, placing one on each of two plates. He tossed a few scraps, bits, and pieces onto the floor and Josie quickly inhaled them. I stood up and walked the few short steps to the table and patted Josie on her back. Kevin seemed to be a good man. Anyone who would give up part of their food to feed a dog and a stranger has integrity and compassion, and that goes a long way in my book. Looking to the table, I saw that the plates held a ham steak, a few salted crackers, and a slice of marbled cheese. It was no feast, but to me, it was a remarkable meal. Glancing over, I noticed the sauce pan held nothing but water that was heated to a slow rolling boil.

"Looks amazing! I guess it's a little late, but... is there anything I can help with?" I asked sincerely.

"Yeah, sure," Kevin replied as he sat the hot skillet on a few bricks that had been set on the floor next to the stove. "Up there, in that cabinet on the left."

24

He said nothing else, and as I opened the cabinet door, I understood why there was no need for explanation. On a slightly dusty, wooden shelf sat several upside down mugs and a jar of instant coffee. I stared at the miracle of java that stood before me and smiled a very cheeky grin. After a moment's pause, I snatched up the two largest mugs and the jar. Turning around, with a smile still on my face, I spoke.

"This is more than I need, but if you are sure that you don't mind sharing, I certainly won't turn it down," I said, as politely as I could.

"Of course, I don't mind. I didn't heat up a pan of water so I could drink coffee in front of you. Besides, it's just instant coffee and rain water I collected out back of the cabin. Real brewed coffee, I might have to think about." He actually smiled at me and I noticed he had, at some point, wiped the camouflage paint from his face.

He had silverware out on the table already and after he filled the mugs with hot water, we made the coffee and began to eat. It was the first real meal I could remember having, and even though it was small, it was more than I had eaten at any one time since before I found myself in the desert. We ate and talked for a long time, making the food last as long as we could. When the meal was well under way, I folded a corner of my cheese slice and slipped it to Josie, who sat loyally at our feet. Our conversation went from how life was before the arrival of the Titans and how drastic things had changed since then, to what all I had been through. There were some things, like Elle, Maddie and some of the extraordinary changes I had experienced that I did not mention, but I told him much of what had happened to me, and he listened intently. By the end of the day, I felt almost as if he considered me as a peer, if not an actual friend... and that restored some of my hope in humanity.

When we were finished, he stacked up the dishes and fumbled for the door. I grabbed for the handle and opened it for him. Following him around the back of the cabin, I spied several buckets and plastic tubs that had been used to capture rain water, in fact, it was still raining. Grabbing a rag that hung on one of the buckets, he began to wash off the plates and flatware. I offered to help, but all that I could really do was to hold the 'clean' dishes when he had finished with them. Once back inside, I put the clean dishes into the cabinet while Kevin stoked the dying embers of the fire.

"Probably just going to let this burn out, to be safer." His voice was concerned. "We don't want too much heat coming off of this place. Out here in the middle of nowhere, we'd stick out like a sore thumb."

"Good point." I agreed. "It is nice while it lasts, though."

"Tomorrow we'll head on to where the others are." He gave me a sideways glance. "Just wait till they get a load of you."

"I guess I have that effect on people when they meet me for the first time. I just hope no one shoots us." I jested, but also meant what I said, considering my past encounters with 'new people'.

We didn't stay up late, and while I can't speak for Kevin, I slept soundly through the night without even a glimpse of a dream. The next morning, Kevin refilled his canteen and packed up very little. He asked if I would carry the cooler, and I was more than happy to oblige. He only carried a small knapsack and his rifle, and Josie, well... Josie wasn't asked to carry anything. When we headed out, Kevin placed a shiny brass lock on the door latch and slipped the key into a small space under the crude window sill. It was a drier day than the day before had been, but with every day that passed the chill of autumn grew. We walked most of the day, only stopping once to snack on a few crackers and pass the canteen. The terrain was not difficult and the patches of woods were only broken by an occasional small field of grasses or wildflowers and weeds. When the day was waning, and the sun was losing it power to light and warm the world around us, we made camp, which really meant nothing more than clearing the ground of sticks and rocks in an area large enough to sleep on.

"As much as I'd like to make it all the way before we stopped, and have a real bed to sleep in, we still have a half a day's hike ahead of us." He said with a thoughtful look on his face as he opened his knapsack. "I thought we'd make better time, but I guess we got a later start than I expected."

"No worries..." I said, matter-of-factly. "I've slept in less comfortable places."

Kevin retrieved two small cellophane-wrapped packets from his pack and tossed one in my direction. My reflexes being what they were, even though I wasn't expecting the throw, allowed me to catch it easily. Much to my surprise, what he had thrown me was an emergency blanket, like the foil ones in a first-aid kit. It was a bit noisy for a minute while we unwrapped and unfolded the 'blankets', but they did keep us warm through the night... along with Josie who had taken turns snuggling up to both of us. The night passed uneventfully and though I did not sleep nearly as well as the night before, I woke with the sunrise and found Kevin already awake and ready to head out.

I jumped into action, folding up the emergency blanket in a very messy and unruly manner and being somewhat embarrassed by its form, handed it to Kevin without really looking him in the eye. Half awake, I rubbed my face and eyes and ran one hand across my head, noticing my hair was as nappy as it had ever been. With eyes aglow, and nappy hair that stood out angrily in non-complimentary directions, I must have looked a frightful mess. Kevin's words came back to me at that moment, 'just wait till they get a load of you'.

"I'm ready when you are." I was as far from ready as I could be, but I was also as ready as I was going to be, out in the wild.

"Okay then... this way." He said as he began the day's journey, not waiting for me or Josie, but knowing that we would soon catch up.

"Half a day left, huh?" I asked as Josie and I jogged through the woods and quickly caught Kevin.

"Maybe less." He smiled. "How lucky, or how brave, do you feel?"

"Considering Josie found me in the middle of the forest and led me to the one person in the wild who fed me and gave me a place to sleep... I feel pretty damn lucky." I put my hand on his shoulder and smiled back.

"Then we will go this way." He directed us to the right and we hiked for less than an hour before we came to a narrow, gravel road. Following it for only thirty minutes, the woods began to thin and we began to see what were once well-tended wheat fields filling the background through the scattered pine and cedar trees. The gravel lane came to an abrupt end at a desolate and wide open paved road. Kevin took the lead and we turned left onto the road. Surrounded by open farmer's fields of yellowing wheat and soybeans, I felt vulnerable. Kevin's remark of 'feeling brave' made sense to me now. I wasn't as worried about myself, considering my last encounter with the alien beings, as I was for the safety of my newly made friends.

The best thing about the open, airy spaces was being able to see anyone or anything coming from a long distance, and while I didn't see anyone, I did see something ahead in our path. Just next to the road ahead was a structure, alone, solitary and plain, but it was definitely a man-made structure.

"What's that?" I asked with a renewed energy.

"Used to be a gas station," Kevin said in a very unemotional tone. "It closed down about two years ago when a convenience store opened up about four miles down the road." He thumbed over his shoulder to indicate that we were walking in the opposite direction from the store.

"Oh..." My excitement went flat, and I had no other reaction. I wondered why we weren't heading towards the store, but I trusted my new traveling companion.

The pavement made for a much easier and swifter traveling than the uneven and obstacled path through the woods. The distance passed underfoot with ease and as the old abandoned gas station drifted by, it appeared unwelcoming and useless to us at this point in our journey. At best, it might offer temporary shelter from a storm or inclement weather which we apparently did not need. A couple of short days ago, I would have given anything to find a shelter like that to sleep in, but now I watched it as we passed it by without hesitation and it shrank behind us.

29

The road rose and climbed steeply uphill. My legs tired and I began to feel the need to rest and maybe have a sip of water before carrying on any further.

"Could I have a drink?" I stopped moving forward and Josie turned back to look at me momentarily before returning to Kevin's side. "I have to catch my breath for a sec."

"Okay, sure... why not." There was frustration in his voice, but he stopped anyway and handed me the canteen.

"Thanks," I said sincerely before I opened the cap and took a mouthful of the foul tasting rainwater. I didn't care. I swished it around in my mouth, forcing it between my teeth and allowed it to soak in and saturate it completely before swallowing it. I wiped my mouth and replaced the cap. After handing it back to Kevin, I followed behind a few paces and my thoughts wandered. The last several days made me wonder what the point of it all was. Yes, I wanted to find Elle, and I felt like maybe I had some 'greater purpose', but still... every passing hour became more and more pointless. Was this life really worth all of the trials and struggles? As I thought back, my most satisfying moment in the past week may very well have been a piece of fried ham and instant coffee... neither of which were really all that good. The space between Kevin, Josie and I had grown and the two of them had stopped at the crest of the hill to wait for me. Kevin half turned and removed his rifle from his shoulder and held it in both hands. It didn't seem as if he had any plan to use it, and I wondered if he was only changing positions out of discomfort. With only a few steps between us, Kevin pointed.

Chapter 3

Serendipity

"It isn't much anymore, but there she is." He said.

As I closed the distance I could begin to see a few houses that were so close, I could sprint to them (if I had the energy) in a few minutes or less. I had to agree, most of what had been there was utterly destroyed and it wasn't much, but there was a row of houses that remained untouched and that gave me some hope of the creature comforts. It was a scene that was not unfamiliar. I had watched as the cabins had been left in splintered ruins and as Barnhill had been trampled underfoot by the same Titan that I had left disabled and 'dying' a week earlier in the mountainous wilderness.

"It looks fantastic... do you think there is any way I could take a bath, or shower?" I felt like I was drooling as the words poured from my lips. "It is pretty torn up... kinda reminds me of Barnhill."

"I'm pretty sure that someone here can get you fixed up with a bath," Kevin said, giving me a curious look of concern, and slinging the rifle back over his shoulder, he reached deep in his knapsack. I had no idea what he was doing until he withdrew a black two-way radio and with a click and the twist of a knob he turned it on.

"Echo, Delta, this is K-9 do you read? Over." he said in a very 'commando' voice.

Static buzzed sharply over the radio speaker and a sudden click cleared the airwaves. "That you Kev? You sound like a damn special forces team leader." The man on the other end of the radio said, sarcastically.

Kevin rolled his eyes, looked at me and pressed the talk button. "Yeah... It's me. I'm coming in... and tell that hard ass, I'm not alone. I can see the house from here and I'm bringing Josie and a refugee in with me."

"You found Josie? That's great! Who's this..." Kevin twisted the knob and cut the man off mid-sentence.

"How did you get those radios to work?" I blurted the question out.

"Yeah... power is a precious commodity these days." He said regretfully. "Two-way rechargeable radios and a gas powered generator...

that's how. But, we only have a few gallons of gas, so we only use it when we have to."

We walked in silence as he stuffed the radio back in his pack and zipped it closed. There were a few houses ahead that could be our destination. On one side of the road, we were traveling was a row of three untouched houses, closest to the road and a few more that were scattered amidst the rubble of houses, trees and autos that had been utterly obliterated by a passing Titan. The first two were nearly identical, bungalow style, homes; one pale blue trimmed in black and one beige with hunter green doors and shutters. The third one was a larger home. It was a one and a half story Cape Cod style. It was white with dark burgundy, board, and batten shutters. The Cape Cod home caught my attention and felt like a place I would call home... I thought to myself, 'That must be the place Kevin was headed... that must be their home base.'

I was focused on the back door, waiting for some sign of his... people... his tribe, when a movement caught my attention from the corner of my eye. From between the two bungalows, two figures emerged, and were not what I expected at all. An elderly couple appeared, waving to us from the edge of the tan home. We turned off of the road and cut through the oversized and overgrown backyard. The couple waited for us in the shadows between the houses. When we approached the old man covered his mouth with his hand and I could see the woman's eyes welling up with tears.

"Don't be afraid. I'm not one of them. I'm not an alien." I knew that was mostly true. I also knew that some part of me, and I wasn't sure how small or how large that part might be, was definitely... alien.

"Dear lord..." The old woman said; her voice soft and kind. "Are you alright?" She looked directly at me, but I wasn't sure if she was directing her question to me or my new acquaintance Kevin.

"Well, of course, he's alright." The old man replied to her before I could. "He's standing right here in front of you, isn't he?"

"Yeah... we're both okay." Kevin almost snarled. "Thanks for asking."

Bursting around the far corner of the Cape Cod, another figure appeared, and I was so dumbfounded that I almost felt lightheaded and weak in the knees, like when you stand up way too quickly and everything goes wonky.

"OH MY GOD! YOU'RE ALIVE!" The familiar voice screamed out in an exhilarated frenzy.

"Elle?... but how?" My quivering voice barely escaped my lips.

The woman that I could not get out of my thoughts and dreams was suddenly rushing into my open and tingling arms. The moment we embraced was miraculous. I felt like I had been given back a part of myself that had been missing since the day I thought I'd lost her. I wanted nothing more and nothing less than to have this very moment never end. Tears escaped my eyes and hers, and it was a beautiful reunion that I had feared would never take place.

"I can't believe I found you!" I finally spoke after a long-anticipated kiss. "How did you get here?"

34

"Silly..." She said in an almost childish way, and taking my head in her hands, looked me straight in the eye. "I never left. I've been waiting for you here and Maddie..." Her words trailed off.

"Maddie? Is she... alright?" I was almost afraid to ask.

Elle shook her head in small but erratic movements, and her eyes had a distant look in them. I held my breath and feared the worst. "She's not doing well at all."

"But she's alive, right?" I finally let out a heavy sigh.

"Yes, for now, but probably not for much longer." A sadness crept into her eyes and slipped back out as new tears that washed away her smile.

"The little girl was touch and go for a couple of days, but then she started to get better." The elderly woman said. "We had been giving her antibiotics and she seemed to be doing pretty good, but she hadn't been up and around but for a day or two when she said her stomach was hurting really bad, and that was what...?"

"Bout four days ago, I guess." The old man interjected.

"About four days ago," The woman continued."...and she's been fading slowly... more and more every day. I don't think she can fight much longer."

"I have to see her." I turned my attention from the woman to Elle.

"You should go now." The old man said, trying to hold his emotions in. "She may not make the night."

Elle took me by the hand and led me around to the front of the beige house. Taking a key from her pocket, she unlocked the door and once inside, locked it behind her. The inside of the home was eerily untouched as if it had been a tidy exhibit in an atomic bomb experiment. I subconsciously kept a tight grip on Elle's hand, wanting to never let go again, and followed her down the hallway to a door that led us to the basement. There were no windows in this subterranean place, lit only by a lantern that hung from the ceiling. Its yellow light cast odd shadows on the peeling and blistered paint of the cinder-block walls. The floor was bare concrete, slick finished and water stained. A small twin sized bed was near one wall and held the tiny, frail body of young Maddie. A middle-aged woman sat at her bedside and a look of shock and disbelief overtook her face when her eyes met mine.

"Good lord!" She said in a loud whisper. "How are you still alive?"

"Lucky, I guess." I didn't know how to respond to her question.

"You probably don't remember me." She stood up and met us half way across the room. "I'm Maryanne. The last time I saw you, was at Ed and Jean's house, across town. You had a bullet hole in your chest the size of my finger and the next thing I knew, we were overrun by those alien people and you just disappeared. Elle said you were okay, but I just thought she was in denial."

Maryanne rambled on and on, and Elle and I skirted around her to get to Maddie. Elle took Maryanne's chair and I knelt down on the cold hard floor. Elle combed the child's hair from her face. She laid so still and her breathing was so shallow, she did not appear to be alive. I took her

36

tiny hand in mine and felt the chill of her touch. Elle caressed her face and her fingers slid down to her neck.

"Her pulse is very faint." Elle's words were filled with emotion.

"She's so cold. Shouldn't she be upstairs where it's warmer?" I posed the question in a reprimanding way as if I knew what was best.

"I'm a nurse, or used to be, and it's best if we don't move her," Maryanne said curtly. "Besides, have you never been in a hospital and complained about how cold it is? It's intentional to slow the growth and spreading of germs."

"Sorry, I'm just a little out of sorts here... everything is just hitting me at once." I tried to apologize to Maryanne. "I appreciate everything you are trying to do to help her."

"It's okay babe, she didn't mean anything by it." It was the first time I had heard Elle call me by a 'pet name' and it was comforting in a distracting way.

"There isn't anything else we can really do for her," Maryanne spoke of little Maddie's state. "But, how did you manage to survive? Can I see your wound?"

"You can look, but you probably won't see anything," I answered.

Her question was also a distraction and I didn't mind satisfying her curiosity. I pulled my dirty and probably unsavory shirt over my head and completely removed it. Maryanne came closer and squinted her eyes searching my chest for the wound or at the very least a scar.

"How in the holy hell..." She whispered to herself, but Elle and I could plainly hear her.

"I guess it's an unusual perk..." I wasn't sure how to explain it. "You see, I had this encounter with one of the alien things that tried to take me over, but it failed. I think it actually died, but somehow in the process, I ended up with an ability to see in the dark, and for a while I had enhanced strength, but I have only eaten a few times since I got shot... one meal really and a few crackers once, and some bugs, and most of that was in the last couple of days. So I've been feeling kinda puny for a while."

"That's all you've had to eat in over two weeks?" Elle broke into our conversation.

"Yeah, but I'm okay," I reassured her. "Anyway... I was getting around to saying that ever since my encounter, I guess I heal up pretty quickly."

Maryanne sat down on the concrete floor beside me and studied my chest. There was not even the slightest sign of a faded scar. Her finger touched the area where I had been shot and she pressed against my muscle to locate some evidence of my injury, but none could be found. She stared at my chest blankly, deep in thought. My attention and Elle's was fixated on little Maddie. The child was cold, pale, limp and seemingly lifeless. I knew she was slipping away all too quickly, and my heart was breaking. Maryanne could see our focus and concern and folded Maddie's blanket down and pulled her loose nightgown up. A patch of gauze was taped in place and discolored with browns and yellows. Maryanne peeled the tape back, exposing her traumatic injury. Several crude stitches were matted in a clump of dried blood and her skin and fatty tissues were pinched and buckled. Unnatural tones of purples and yellows surrounded the blackened wound, and the smell of infection and death oozed from it like the yellowy puss that seeped through the stitches.

"I have a thought... an idea," Maryanne spoke as quickly as the thoughts that bombarded her.

"What?" Elle drilled her for more. "Speak up, woman. What idea?"

"It could possibly save her life... but most likely it would kill her." Maryanne stumbled over her words.

"You wanna tell me what the hell you're talking about?" Elle was losing her patience, but it wasn't anything that Maryanne had said or done, it was only Elle's stress escaping through her lips.

"I don't know on what level the alien encounter has changed Tanner, but it is on a very basic level... possibly cellular." She began to explain. "If whatever has caused those changes is in his blood, and we inject some of his blood into her, maybe it would begin to multiply in her bloodstream and throughout her body, and she might heal herself in the same way that Tanner has."

"But..." I knew there was more... there was always a 'but'.

"But..." She took in a deep breath. "It might not have that effect at all, it's a very long shot at best... just a guess. Wishful thinking, really, and if it doesn't work it could be a death sentence."

"Why?" Elle's voice was less harsh but still demanded more answers.

"Well, we have no way of checking, and unless we know both blood types, it would be a huge risk. If the types don't match, the most likely result would be that Tanner's blood would begin to coagulate in Maddie's veins, forming blood clots. Those clots would probably cause pulmonary embolisms and strokes, which in this case would, without a doubt, lead quickly to her death." Maryanne rubbed her hand across her face and covered her mouth in recognition of the choices that lay before us.

"I see..." Elle said solemnly. "What happens to her if it goes wrong, and what are her chances if we do nothing?"

"Considering her current state, if it went badly, she simply wouldn't wake up... and if we do nothing, I can't be sure, but I think she may have an infection in her blood, and if that's the case, she won't wake up either." Maryanne's prognosis was dismal at best. "If I am right, the difference could be as little as a few hours of unconscious life for her."

"Then, my suggestion is that we spend the next hour with her, saying our goodbyes, and then we try it, but it is not my decision." I took the cowards way out and left the tough choice up to someone else.

"You're right." Elle's immediate agreement was unexpected. "Either way, we should spend our time with her telling her how much she is loved, and saying good-bye."

"I'll leave you two to it then." Maryanne stood up. "I have to get some things prepped for the procedure."

"Alright, we'll be right here," I answered back.

Elle and I stayed by Maddie's side and talked about all we had been through together, every moment that Maddie had lightened or made us smile, and what a special and beautiful person she was. It was a conversation that we included her in as if she was awake and participating. I told the tale of my weeks away, descriptively detailing the most minute facts, to Maddie but Elle listened intently to every single word. Her eyes widened when I spoke of taking over the Titan and how every Taker began to chant 'Unify' as I deserted them. This was the first and only time we had ever heard of a Taker speaking. I spoke very lightheartedly about how Josie had found me, lost in the wilds and had led me back to her and Elle. The time passed quickly with no response from Maddie.

Running her fingers through the child's hair, Elle spoke. "Her fever is spiking. We need to do this if we're going to. Her little body won't take much more."

"Alright." After rambling for over forty minutes, I spoke the only word I could muster.

At that very moment, we heard the sound of the door opening, rushed footsteps across the floor upstairs and then on the basement steps. Maryanne appeared and crossed the room to where we sat, carrying a canvas, travel bag over her shoulder and was followed closely by Angie who carried a small folding TV dinner tray. Angie pushed her way in between Maddie and I and placed the unfolded tray across her mid-section, covering it with a piece of torn, white bed-sheet that smelled faintly like alcohol. Maryanne opened her shoulder bag and began removing stacks of gauze, rubbing alcohol, a handful of latex gloves, several syringes, and medical tape, placing each item in its place on the tray.

"I guess it's time," Maryanne said as she pulled another chair up next to the bed. "Elle, could you give us some room and let Tanner have your seat?"

"Sure." Elle nodded and spoke quietly.

She stood up and crossed behind me, sitting on the floor at the foot of Maddie's bed. Angie took one of the pieces of gauze and doused it with rubbing alcohol until it was nearly dripping wet while Maryanne searched my arm for a candidate vein. She flipped my arm over and held my hand in hers.

"This will work." She said softly, rubbing the thick and obvious veins on the back of my hand. "I don't have the supplies I need, so I am probably going to have to stick you a few times and draw one syringe of blood at a time."

I nodded in acknowledgment. With a glance from Maryanne, Angie took the alcohol soaked gauze and scrubbed the back of my hand. The scent of the evaporating rub stung my nostrils and I prepared myself for the possibilities that were only minutes away. She tossed the gauze to the floor and grabbed a second one from the tray, soaking it and cleansing Maddie's inner forearm. She slid the tray down over Maddie's thighs and gently wiped the area around her putrid wound.

"We may know in a few minutes, I think, if this is going to work or not," Maryanne said as she opened the sterile packaging of the first syringe.

She pinched the skin on the back of my hand several times and then I felt the burning prick of the needle penetrating my skin and vein. Her hands were shaky and I watched as the sweat beaded on her forehead and the blood filled the syringe. She put one of the small gauze squares over the injection spot and slowly removed the syringe.

"That went well. Here, hold this in place tight." She said, and I did as instructed. "Here Angie... Help me out here."

She gestured towards the lantern. Angie removed the lantern from its hanger, turned the knob to intensify the glowing mantles and held the light close to Maddie's pale and spindly forearm. Using her wrist, Maryanne wiped the sweat from her brow and squinted through her librarian style reading glasses. She squeezed the child's arm at the elbow and searched for a vein. A series of exasperated sighs and failed jabs and Maryanne finally found a vein to accept the needle.

"Okay." She said. "Everybody... pray. Pray real hard." and with that, she cautiously and hesitantly squeezed the plunger with her trembling hand.

"Bandage." She directed Angie as she removed the steely needle from the girl's arm. Angie wiped the puncture point with a sterile pad and placed an adhesive bandage over it.

"Do we do that all again now?" I asked, remembering the procedure she had explained earlier.

"Not yet." She sat back on her chair and removed her latex gloves. "If she doesn't have a bad reaction, we will repeat the process a few times."

"So what do we do now?" Elle asked. Her voice had a hint of worry and frustration that shown through her tough girl exterior.

"Well, now we wait." Maryanne cocked her head to the side and pitifully faked a smile.

Chapter 4

A New Beginning

A wind-up, alarm clock sat on a small and mostly empty bookshelf in the corner of the basement room. Both had gone completely unnoticed until now. The four of us sat silently, surrounding the dying child and the ticking of the clock seemed to grow exponentially louder and slowed with every passing second. Just over a half an hour had passed and I couldn't stand the silent stillness any longer.

"She isn't getting any better. How long do we have to wait?" I shattered the quiet of the basement gathering.

"There may not be anything noticeable yet, but that's a good thing," Maryanne said. "She hasn't reacted badly either. Let's give it a while longer." A tear welled up in her eyes as she spoke, and the silence overtook the room again as we watch the motionless child and waited as the eternal minutes passed.

"I'm not a hundred percent sure..." Elle said with surprising lightness in her voice as she took the girl's face in her hands. "But I think her fever is breaking."

Maryanne wedged her way between Maddie and I, like a Black Friday shopper trying to reach the bargain of the year before anyone else. She placed the back of her hand on the child's forehead and after a few seconds moved it down just below her jawline. Her eyes closed tight in intense concentration.

Her eyes opened wide and her lips curled up at the corners. "Her pulse is getting stronger... at least, it's not as shallow as it has been."

"So, do we give her another dose of... you know..." Angie danced around the 'elephant in the room', and shot her eyes from Maryanne to me several times quickly. I nearly chuckled.

"I suppose we could," Maryanne answered her dodgy question. "We don't know for sure if it was the injection that helped, or if she is just having a good minute. Her fever could spike again anytime and cause her vitals to go haywire."

"Maybe we should wait." I surprised everyone in the room with my opinion. "If she continues to get better, we don't have to take any unnecessary risks, and if she takes a turn for the worse, we are set-up and ready to repeat the procedure at a moment's notice."

"I think that's not altogether a bad idea." Elle agreed with me and the ladies couldn't argue.

Maryanne called Angie over to the other side of the room. The two had a short conversation so hushed that I could not hear anything but wispy sounds. When they finished, Angie took off up the stairs and Maryanne grabbed the lantern, gave it a few pumps which brightened its glow, and returned to her seat. Elle stood up to stretch her legs, and I motioned her over. Taking her by the hand, I pulled her onto my lap and held her close to me.

"It's going to be okay," I whispered in her ear and she slumped against me, hugging my neck.

I drew in her scent like an animal on the hunt. It was intoxicating and Maddie's improved condition eased my mind enough to wander back to our one night of uninhibited passion. I remembered every detail of that night, every sensation, and every sound, and I could hardly believe that nearly a month had passed. Maybe it was just me, or maybe it was the time spent apart, but something about Elle was different. Maybe her personality or attitude had changed because of Maddie, but I didn't think that was it. This was something deeper... something on a primal level... maybe it was her scent or a vibe or pheromone that was slightly different, but something about her was different. Something about her was... new, and I found that both exhilarating and frightening.

I was lost in the moment until a sudden sound distracted me and brought me back to the present. I heard the door and a herd of footsteps on the floor above us. There were several people moving about upstairs and Elle, Maryanne and I took notice. Maryanne and Elle seemed unconcerned by the commotion and I trusted their reaction.

"Any idea what's going on up there?" Elle asked Maryanne.

"Yes, I do... dinner." She smiled. "Why don't you two run up and eat. Angie can bring a plate down to me."

"No, you go on up and eat. We'll stay here." I spoke for both of us, without asking.

"Fine. If you're gonna be that way about it." She said in a huff, but I had a feeling she wasn't being completely serious when she jumped up and trotted upstairs.

"I hope you don't mind," I whispered in Elle's ear.

"Of course not. I was thinking the same thing." She kissed my forehead. "Well, I was going to offer to stay and let you and her go up first."

"That doesn't surprise me one bit," I smiled.

The commotion upstairs didn't quite like I had expected, instead, it moved from one area to another and then onto the stairs. Before we knew what was happening, we were joined by six others. Maryanne and Angie, Ed and Jean, Kevin and Jimmy all crowded into the room. Altogether, including Maddie, there were nine of us and the empty and quiet room became filled with the echo of murmured voices and the smell of a home cooked meal.

"Everyone wanted to come by and see the girl," Angie said, handing Elle a plate. "Maryanne and I though her improvement was a cause to celebrate. We haven't had much reason to do that lately."

Another plate was passed to Angie, who passed it on to me. Elbow macaroni and tomatoes, fried potatoes and green beans cooked with chunks of ham covered the plate and I could not wait to fill my belly again. I held the plate under my nose and inhaled the tantalizing aroma.

"We just wanted to come down and say hello again and say thank you for trying to help the little girl," Ed said, with his arm around Jean, giving her an elated squeeze.

"Yeah..." Kevin added. "We won't stay. It's probably best not to fill the room with people... her trying to get better and all."

Jimmy said nothing, but I could feel the disdain of his stare. He was the first to leave the room, followed by Kevin. Ed and Jean soon followed them and then Angie. We were left with Maryanne, who had brought down her own plate. We ate and talked about so many different things. I learned that Maryanne had gone to med school when she was in her early twenties and was a registered nurse in the nearby city of Bakersfield before the appearance of the Titans and Elle had been studying dance and was a former marine, having served for four years and had enlisted right out of high school.

"I had a professor in college who was a biochemist. He would have loved to have just one drop of your blood to study. He used to talk about working with a geneticist to try to find the particular DNA code or sequence that may have caused a predisposition to cancer. The two of them... well probably dozens of the top researchers in the field, could make careers out of studying you..." She paused awkwardly embarrassed. "I'm sorry. I just made it sound like you were some science experiment. I didn't mean..."

"No need to apologize. I know exactly what you meant, I think." I tried not to assume. "And honestly, I'd be fascinated to learn more about me, or at least about the me that I've become."

The bed shook erratically. Maddie seemed to be having a seizure and before we could even react, her body went rigid and her back and neck arched in such a way that the only parts of her that still touched the bed were her feet and the crown of her head. Her arms splayed out to her sides at ninety-degree angles and hung over the sides of the twin bed. We were bewildered and had no idea what we could do. One last single convulsion and her tiny frame went limp on the bed.

"Maddie!" Elle cried out in anguish.

Maryanne dropped her plate and it struck the unforgiving concrete floor and shattered, sending the remains of her meal and her fork scattering in all directions. She leapt to the bedside and grabbing Maddie's wrist in one hand, laid her ear against the child's chest. Elle and I heard Maryanne's audible sigh as her tension eased and she relaxed without changing her position.

Raising her head from the girl's chest, she calmly said, "I think she just might make it through this. Her heart and her breathing are sounding stronger than they have since she lost consciousness."

The day was coming to an end and we decided to take shifts, sitting with Maddie. Elle volunteered for the first shift, and I followed

Maryanne upstairs. She led me down the hallway to one of the three bedrooms. I gave her a long overdue hug and let my gratitude pour from me and she graciously accepted it. The full sized bed was incredibly comfortable and the sheets were fresh and crisp. I soon fell into a deep, near comatose, sleep and didn't wake up until I felt someone shaking my shoulder.

"Your turn, if you're up to it." Maryanne's kind voice pulled me from my peaceful slumber.

Much to my surprise, I found Elle curled up next to me, in her own world of dreams. I climbed out of bed and gently kissed her cheek before slipping from the room and heading down to our makeshift infirmary. Across the room, under the dim glow of soft lantern light, lay Maddie. Her tiny frame lay motionless beneath a pallid sheet and her hair was a matted mess, not unlike anyone who had been bedridden for days, or longer. The odd lighting of the lantern washed away the distinct colors and I could not be sure if her cheeks were truly flushed, or if it was only an illusion, but I quickly found the answer.

"She hasn't stirred at all, and her fever seems to be returning," Maryanne said in a hushed whisper as if waking Maddie were a bad thing.

"I guess that's not good, huh?" I contemplated the possibility that our experiment was a failure. "Maybe we could try again in the morning if she keeps getting worse again."

"Come here..." She motioned with her hand for me to follow her as she crossed the room and knelt at the child's bedside. "Look."

Gently and unobtrusively, she raised the sheet and folded it back on itself. With the care and precision of an expert defusing a bomb, she exposed the gauze bandaging from the girl's midsection. Taking the lantern in hand, she illuminated the horrid wound. My mouth hung open at the sight of it. The bruising was perceptibly lighter and at some point, Maryanne must have removed the crude sutures. The hole that had been torn through Maddie's abdomen was closed and the scar appeared like one that was years old and had been well cared for by a professional. Maryanne smiled.

"You, my dear, are a godsend... and this child..." She teared up as she spoke. "Well, she's nothing short of a miracle."

"I'm just a guy who did what any other part alien, amnesiac would have done after being shot, riding an alien craft across the mountain and nearly starving after two weeks in the wilderness before being rescued by a dog would have done," I grinned at the middle aged woman and saw the glow of my eyes reflecting in hers. "Anyways... I would have walked across the whole country and back to save Maddie or Elle, but really, you were the one with the brilliant idea and the medical training to make it happen."

"Anyone who's ever had blood drawn could have done what I did. It had a lot more to do with you than me, but thank you just the same." She wrapped me in a warm and genuinely heartfelt hug, and my arms returned the sentiment, but I knew that she deserved a lot more credit than she was giving herself.

Maryanne had gone upstairs to sleep and the rest of the night passed slowly and with no real change in Maddie's condition, except for the rise and fall of her temperature. Her temp rose until her hair was damp with sweat and her forehead felt like it was on fire, only to quickly plummet to the point that her cheeks paled and became cold and clammy. It was a roller-coaster for several hours and was spiking dangerously high when a sound on the stairs announced the morning arrival of Elle. She was a beautiful mess with her hair in tangles and nothing on but a man's oversized, flannel, button-down shirt and a sleepy smile. She tussled her hair and with an open mouthed yawn, stretched her arms upwards, causing the shirttails to lift and nearly reveal herself to me.

"How long have you been sitting down here in the dark?" She caught me off guard with her question.

"Good morning to you too." My sarcasm caused me to grin, even though she probably couldn't see it. "I really have no idea. I mean... I guess the lantern must have faded out and I just didn't notice."

"No, I guess you wouldn't" She reached out to 'feel her way' to where I was. "Keep talking... tell me about Maddie."

"I think she's going to be okay. She's been running a fever some, but the gunshot is looking a lot better." I watched as her hands waved in front of her and her bare feet drug across the cold floor. "Be careful of the table... just to your left. Don't wanna stub your toe."

She was so close I could hear her nervous breaths. It was like playing Marco-polo without the water. I stood up and took her in my arms and buried my face in the tangled mess of her raven hair. I could sense an undeniable emotion that we both shared. It frightened me, probably more than it should have. I reached up and tucked her hair behind her ear and gently taking her chin in my hand, kissed her ever so softly.

"Tanner I... Well, I have been thinking this for a while, and maybe it's partly because I didn't know if I would see you again... maybe I'm over thinking this and making more of this than it really is..." She hesitated, fumbling her words and for the first time ever, almost seeming introverted. "Tanner... I..."

"Ms. Elle? That you?" The frail and parched voice behind me saved Elle, just in the nick of time. I could not speak, and my arms went numb and fell to my sides like they weighed a thousand pounds. I crumpled into the chair that sat directly behind me and I could not turn or look away from Elle.

"Ohhhh-oh-oh..." Her voice stuttered and she raised her quivering hand to cover her mouth. Rubbing her pointer finger under her nose and sniffling in deeply, she spoke. "Yes baby girl, it's me."

I did my best to hold my emotions in, but Elle could not contain her tears, and willingly let them flow, noisily blubbering with unbridled joy. She flailed her arms around and made her way to the floor where she openly sobbed. "I lost you both, but now... now you both came back to me..."

"It's okay Ms. Elle. You don't have to cry." The child's voice was barely a whisper.

"You want me to get you a drink of water?" I looked over to Maddie. She nodded silently, and that's when it hit me. She knew Elle was there, in the pitch blackness of the basement room with no windows. My first thought was that she had recognized her voice, but when she nodded to me, she looked directly into my eyes, and I could see. Her eyes were like snow-globes filled with glitter. Sparkling flecks of pale green starlight shone through the darkness, and I knew somehow, when all of the odds were against us, suddenly, this girl was about to change everything.

***

The days flew by quickly, and little Maddie grew stronger with each passing hour. No sign of Titan or Taker had been seen or heard and our days slipped into a routine of collecting water from the nearby stream, preparing meals to feed the small, mismatched clan of friends and the everyday chores and pleasures of bathing, brushing teeth, and shaving... how I enjoyed being clean and shaven after weeks of being lost in the wild. Elle and I became like adoptive parents to Maddie, reading to her or with her, teaching her basic elementary skills mixed with a few survival techniques. We taught her how to used some basic, everyday items to collect morning dew and even the smallest amount of misty rain water. Ed was more of a help than I would have anticipated. Using simple paper and colored pencils he was able to draw, quite artistically, several species of plants with edible roots, berries, grains or even leaves and stalks. He drew very realistic and almost 3-D sketches of leaves of trees that would, in season, bear edible fruit or nuts.

Weeks passed, and our simple lives were good. The man who had brought me back to Barnhill, Kevin, would sometimes bring in animals he had hunted, mostly rabbits, but once he had brought back a small mule deer. We ate fairly well, had a freshwater stream within walking distance and some of us had become complacent. I had not, but I had become quite comfortable, finding a house that Elle, Maddie and I had claimed as our own and enjoying a very rudimentary family life. There was also a quiet and near constant voice within my head that continually reminded me that I had a greater purpose than just this simple existence. The days were growing shorter and cooler. Autumn was approaching, and winter would soon be upon us. I had a destiny to fulfill and it was time to have *the talk* with Elle, Maddie and the half a dozen other friends that had become our new tribe.

Chapter 5

Cool Change

I had spoken to Maryanne, Angie and Jean and Ed and had suggested that we have a feast. It had been quiet for weeks and I had an announcement to make. All agreed and we announced it to the remaining few a couple of days before the planned event. We had lost track of the days, but Ed had tried to keep up by the phases of the moon and a wall calendar. According to his calculations, it was mid-October. Elle, Maryanne, Ed and I had decided that the day we held our feast, which was the day after the new moon, we would mark on our calendar as

Wednesday, October the 14[th.] From that day forward, our tribe and any descendants that may come after us, no matter where we were, would celebrate the date as our own private holiday... a day set aside to celebrate new beginnings... our Genesis Day.

Kevin had spent most of his days in the woods, hunting and keeping a lookout. More recently, Elle and I had noticed he was spending more and more time with Angie. They had become somewhat of an item. The day and evening before the Genesis Feast, as we had all begun to call it, Kevin had ventured deep into the forest and spent countless hours waiting for just the right game to wander along.

My nervous excitement had awakened me while the stars still filled the sky. I slipped outside and took a seat in a patio chair at the back of our house. That sounded oddly comforting to think... our house. I contemplated the idea as I stared blankly into the night sky and the countless pinpoints of starlight. Being a new moon, the stars and the Milky Way shone crystal clear. I could see the varied colors, sizes, and intensities of the stars and the planets in our solar system. I began to wonder about our intrusive visitors and which star was the home of their planet... if they were from another planet. Perhaps they were from some other dimension that physicists had not yet even thought of or dreamed up. I wondered how I might play into the whole scheme of things, and just why I was 'chosen' by this Moro-Dan, the commander of the Pale Titan. I had so much on my mind and my decision to leave would not be an easy thing to announce, especially to Elle and Maddie.

I thought long and hard about my uncertain future and as the sun came up on our newly created holiday, Kevin appeared on the horizon. He trudged towards our leftover suburb slowly and I decided to meet him halfway. As the distance between us shrank, it became clear to me that he was arduously dragging something behind him. I jogged out to meet him and my soul was overjoyed when I saw his prize. Dragging behind him was a fully dressed, young wild hog. It probably didn't weigh a hundred pounds, which was perfect. It would cook up nice and tender and there would not be as much waste as if it had been a huge boar. I took the rope from Kevin to give him a break, but I found it to be no work whatsoever to drag behind me the rest of the way back.

A fire was built, and when it was well prepared, the pig was put on a spit and began to roast. Our tiny patch in this great big world was all abuzz with preparations for our big feast. The house that Elle, Maddie and I called home had been chosen to host the celebration since it had an open floor plan between the kitchen, dining room, and living room. While the kitchen was a nice place for preparations, like all other kitchens, it was useless for cooking. Two charcoal grills had been set up near the oblong fire that the pig was roasting over. The bottom of the grills were filled with hot coals and after the grates were in place, they became the stove tops that were used to cook all of the side dishes. Large pans were filled with canned sweet corn, green beans, carrots, and potatoes. Mrs. Jean even whipped up a batch of homemade fried bread.

It was nearly 4:30 before the wild hog was finished and the tables were set. It was a feast to behold and every one of us helped in some way. Even little Maddie was put on the task of tending to the simmering vegetables at times and helped with the place settings. Festive cloths covered the tables and the places were set with the finest dinner plates and silverware. During her scavenging, Angie had recovered several candlesticks and glass holders in one of the houses. She had also found two undiscovered four-pound bags of sugar and even though we usually had not splurged, this was an extra special occasion, so two large pitchers of sweet tea were made. When all was finished, and everyone was prepared, we gathered together around the tables.

"Could everyone join hands?" Ed asked, and most everyone answered with replies of 'yes' or 'sure' or nodded and smiled. Jimmy had tried to squeeze in next to Elle, but with me on one side, and Maddie on the other, he found himself holding the hand of a seven-year-old on his left and Mrs. Jean on his right. His face had a sour look, but no one paid him much attention and eventually, as Ed spoke, his scowl turned to a smile.

"Dear Lord, we gather here today to give thanks for our lives and our friendships. Today is a day for new beginnings and future blessings that we have not even thought of. We thank you for bringing these three new friends into our lives and the wonderful gift they have brought to us. Once we were alone in this world, but now we have hope that there are other people, other places that continue to survive, and even thrive as we once did. Thank you also for the gift of the, what did you call them? ... Titans? It was through their appearance and the strange changes they have brought, that we find ourselves truly grateful for the smallest of blessings. Thank you for this abundant meal, this 'Genesis Feast', and bless it, and bless us... so that we may one day have peace on Earth. Amen." As Ed raised his head and opened his eyes, his words were echoed with 'amens' from all who had gathered together.

The food was passed and plates were filled and refilled as our lighthearted conversations filled the air with sounds that I could only pretend to remember. There had not been a time that I had felt this much camaraderie since... well, maybe ever. When the sun set and the sky outside darkened, the candlelight sparkling in Elle's eyes caught my attention over and over again. I did not want this moment to end and I dreaded what was coming next. I tried to put it out of my mind until the time was right and enjoy the evening with my new friends... friends that felt more like family. We had finished with the meal, but sat around the tables nibbling at the leftovers, reluctant to end the wonderful celebration we had created. Everyone told stories, joked and laughed and even the tiny giggles of Maddie raised everyone's spirits far beyond our expectations. I was about to make my announcement when Jean beat me to the punch. She had an announcement of her own.

"I was saving these for something special, and I don't suppose it is going to get any more special than tonight." She grinned, picking up a small rectangular box that had been set off to the side on a small decorative table, and covered in an old dishtowel.

"Saving?" Ed teased. "You mean hoarding, don't ya?"

"You just hush, or you'll get *none*!" Jean poked at him with playful sarcasm. She removed the dishtowel and the box lid and revealed a full box of assorted chocolates. Her revelation was met with oohs and aahs and groans of anticipated pleasure.

"Well, I guess I have a little something for us too then," Ed said as he and Jean disappeared into the next room. They returned carrying armloads of actual wine glasses and while Jean passed them out, Ed disappeared once again and returned with two bottles of a fairly nice white zinfandel. The first bottle was uncorked and when the glasses were filled, Jimmy stood up and spoke.

"I guess I'd like to make a toast." He paused for a moment as everyone raised their glasses, including Maddie, whose glass was filled with tea. "To friends, n-n-n-new and old, and to learning that w-w-w-we should always be thankful for what we have, and not be jealous of what we d-don't. Cheers"

"Here, here!" Ed cheerfully replied along with several other echoed 'cheers'.

It wasn't long before the second bottle was opened and glasses had been refilled. My cheerful disposition had quickly grown somber. Though I toyed with the idea of procrastinating, the inevitable moment was upon me. I stood.

"Thank you to everyone. You are all special to me in your own ways, and no matter what the future may hold, I can promise you this- I will never forget any of you and I will fondly remember you, and often." My words were met with looks of confusion. "This day, the day of The Genesis Feast, is a day to celebrate new beginnings and there is one more new beginning that I have been planning to announce tonight." Elle reached up and took my hand in hers, unsure of what I may be preparing to say. "I have a destiny that was partially revealed when I left in the Titan... however many weeks ago, and I must leave again to fulfill that destiny. I don't want to leave such wonderful and admirable friends, but I feel that I must."

My hands trembled and Elle tried to comfort me with gentle touches, stroking my arm and still holding my hand. The room was filled with a thousand silent questions, spoken by the eyes of all of the onlookers. Many of them did not want me to leave, and some may have been slightly indifferent, but every single one of them, including Elle, had not expected my news. I felt they were all asking 'why?' without saying a word, and I felt that they deserved an explanation.

"When I was inside of the Titan, I was confronted by its alien commander and I was 'told' that I was the key to finding the 'rogue Titan'... the Pale Titan. Then, when we physically touched, it... died." I explained in the simplest of terms. "The next thing I knew, I was in control of the Titan and when I decided I need to come back to find Elle, I left the Titan behind, and the Takers began to follow me."

"Wow... that's incredible!" Kevin finally broke the silence of the circle of my friends.

"How'd ya get away?" Jimmy chimed in with his curiosity.

"I didn't have to. They weren't coming after me. They were following me. When I thought to myself 'I wish they would stop' they did." I thought I must have sounded like an egotistical liar, but my tribe of friends did not perceive me in that way whatsoever.

"So they just did what you wanted them to do?" Angie asked rhetorically. "You should have let them follow you here. I could have used the help with the laundry and dish washing."

"That woulda been a bad idea," Kevin interjected. "Probably would have got him shot."

"That is amazing." Elle finally spoke up, but she seemed lost and almost apathetic. "And this is why you need to leave? Because of a bunch of zombie alien people who'll do your bidding?"

"No... it's because when I was almost out of their sight, I heard something. They were chanting over and over... 'unify', and I couldn't help but think about Bobby and how he came back to you to say good-bye to you." I looked deep into the rich brown eyes of the woman that had become my reason for living. "If there is some part of humanity left inside of the Takers and the Ahsusha, maybe I can help them find it..." My words trailed off and I quietly repeated myself without thinking. "...maybe I can help them."

"Then I'm coming with you." Elle subconsciously tightened her grip on my hand. "And don't you even think about arguing with me." She smiled a halfhearted smile.

"Me too!" Maddie announced that she was still part of our conversation and paying more attention than I had realized. "Can I ride in one of those Titans too?" Her innocence was heartbreakingly refreshing. I did not know how to respond to her plea, but, fortunately, I didn't have to.

"No sweetie. You need to stay here and help Mrs. Jean and Mr. Ed, and you need to learn everything you can from Maryanne. She can teach you all about how to take care of people and nurse them back to health." I could hear Elle's heart breaking as she spoke.

"But I want to stay with you," Maddie whined.

"I know baby. I want to stay with you too... but I'll tell you what..." Elle searched her soul for what to say next.

"What?" Maddie coaxed her impatiently.

"I'll come back for you." Elle's eyes welled with tears.

"We'll come back..." I reassured her.

"Pinky promise... or it doesn't count." Maddie's whine turned into a sorrowful plea for some guarantee that we would be together again.

"Pinky promise." Elle choked out through her sniffling tears, and then the two locked pinky fingers and shook them.

It was more than Elle could stand and she grabbed up the little girl and hugged her like she may never see her again... and we both knew that was probably more likely than our return. Elle and the glitter-eyed child slipped off to the sofa and talked at great length, about what, I'm not sure, but I believe Elle was convincing her that everything would turn out for the best if she would let us leave. There may have been a lot of discussion about Elle keeping her promise to return as well, but by the time the dinner tables were cleared and the dishes were being washed, Elle had brought Maddie in to pass out good night hugs to everyone. She seemed to be at peace with our separating and I was very proud of this little girl for being so grown up about such a difficult thing to bear.

"Come here you!" I called to her and she scurried over to me. I stooped down and let her jump into my open arms. "I promise I'll bring Ms. Elle back to you," I whispered in her ear as I hugged her tightly.

"I know," She said very matter-of-factly. "Go where it's warmer and I'll see you all in the water."

I gave her a smile though her words sounded odd, yet confident and intentional. "Someone is getting sleepy. Are you sure you were drinking tea?" I teased.

"Let me help you get ready for bed," Maryanne said cheerily. "I don't want to do any more dishes anyway." She stuck her tongue out and made a silly face at Maddie, pulling out one more giggle.

A few minutes passed and Maryanne poked her head into the dining room, around the corner from the hallway. "Someone is asking for Mr. Tanner and Ms. Elle to tuck them in." Elle and I made our way into the child's room and found Maddie snuggled up under a thick paisley comforter and propped up on a fat feather pillow. A candle lit the room dimly and brought dancing shadows to life on the walls around us. The pale green sparkles in Maddie's sad eyes caught mine and I couldn't look away. Elle sat on the bed next to her and I knelt next to her on the floor. I combed Maddie's hair from her face with my fingers.

"Everything is going to be alright, isn't it?" I asked and Elle shot me a stern look, wondering why I would ask a child such a troubling question.

"Even better than alright," Maddie smiled. "Lots of us will meet at the water."

"What does that mean, honey?" Elle asked as if she were trying to unravel one of our life's great mysteries.

"I dunno... I just know." Maddie shrugged her shoulders and then sat up and hugged Elle tight around her belly. Quietly she whispered. "I'll see you by the water."

With the candles out and Maddie fast asleep, our tribe of friends scattered to their own houses. Elle and I had found ourselves completely alone in the house we had claimed. It wasn't that much different than any other night, as Maddie was a sound sleeper, but it definitely felt different. The night found us in the uninhibited throes of passionate love. Perhaps it was the nip in the night air, with autumn well underway, or maybe it was knowing that there was little chance of being interrupted by the tiny voice of a seven-year-old. I wasn't sure at that moment, but I knew there was something amazingly special happening. Elle and I had what was probably the most romantic encounter ever. We had connected on levels that did not need words or lights. Every touch was electrifying and whether it was the touch of a hand, a kiss or bare arms wrapped around the bare skin of each other, when skin touched skin, there was a sensation I could only describe as wondrously magical.

The night culminated with my exhausted arms holding Elle's quivering body close. A million thoughts crossed my mind and a million romantic things to say darted in and out of my thoughts, but all I could manage were four simple words. "Elle, I love you."

"I love you too, my sexy man," Elle said gratuitously as she caressed my chest and nuzzled her face against my shoulder. "I've been kinda wanting to tell you that, and something else, for a while now. It just never seemed like the right time, but now that we're leaving..."

"Well..." I tried to coax her along. "Don't keep me in suspense," I smiled out loud.

"Ummm..." She hesitated. "I kinda think, maybe... I'm not really 100% positive..."

"Come on!" I spluffed jokingly.

"There is this chance that maybe... I'm pregnant." She cringed as if she thought I might be upset or even angry.

"Really? I'm gonna be a...." It suddenly hit me. We hadn't made love until after I had my life-altering encounter with the Ahsusha. *'What could this mean?'* I thought. "...a dad."

I began to realize that sleep was something I had experienced the night before, and no matter how busy our day had been, how stuffed I had been after our feast, or how exhausted I was... sleep would probably be something I would not experience on this particular night. Heading out into the unforgiving and now untamed world seemed like it may not be such a wise idea. I wondered how long Elle would be able to travel in her new condition. The nutritional needs of a pregnant woman would most likely far exceed what we would scrounge to eat 'on the road'. I did not strike up that conversation as I knew it would take us well into the morning hours, debating whether or not we should embark on our adventure, or whether I should go alone... the latter would probably be the best choice, but I knew that was an argument I did not want to have. So, I waited until morning to bring up our options.

Chapter 6

Independence

Dawn came early, considering I had only fallen asleep an hour or two earlier. Elle, on the other hand, had slept hard and deep, and even snored lightly for a while after she first fell asleep. Popping out of bed like a bunny chased by a hunting dog, she began to whirl around the room, pulling two oversized, hiker style backpacks from the closet and sorting through clothes to decide what to pack.

"Are you ready for the big day?" She asked as if we were heading out on vacation.

"Maybe we should rethink this whole idea of leaving, what with you being pregnant and all," I said, slowly dragging myself to the edge of the bed.

"No way," Elle stated firmly. "I'm not even 100% sure I'm pregnant, and besides, who knows what we'll find out there. Maybe there is another town that hasn't been affected, with a clinic, or hospital or something. If nothing else, surely we'll come across a pharmacy where I can get some vitamins and stuff... you know, like prenatal." It was obvious she had thought this through and her mind was set.

"You have a good point, but what if six months from now, we are out there somewhere and we are overrun by Takers? How could you fight them off? Or what if we end up lost with no food or water, what then?" I tried to argue, completely in vain... this *was* a woman after all.

"Okay..." As soon as the words left her beautiful lips, I knew I was in trouble. "What if we stay here and the Takers come back? What if we have a really bad winter and I get pneumonia? Or what if we can't find enough food for NINE PEOPLE to survive all winter... WHAT THEN?" I could tell she wasn't truly angry, but it was her way of showing me that just because we felt comfortable in the ruins of Barnhill, we weren't any safer than we were anywhere else.

"Point taken." I quickly ended my poor attempt to persuade her to stay. "I guess we had better pack up what we can carry and get on our way. Get as far as we can while we still have daylight." Some would say I had given up or given in, but I chose to look at it as having changed my point of view. "You know the weather will probably get worse and colder... and the daylight hours will get shorter, leaving us more time that we are vulnerable to be seen by their thermal vision... or whatever it is they have." I knew exactly how it worked, but it was easier to not have to go into detail right at that moment.

"Of course, I know all of that. Why do you think I am up packing while you are still sitting there naked on the side of the bed." She smiled a devilish grin.

"Okay... okay, I'm moving." I found a bit of hidden energy, quickly dressed and began to pick out a few clothes (mostly socks and underwear, but also a couple of rolled up shirts and pants) to pack in the bottom of my backpack.

While we packed up what we could, a knock came at the front door. Elle and I stopped our packing to see who it was and what they wanted so early in the morning. We assumed it was someone either wanting to help or not wanting to miss seeing us off. It was both. I opened the door and Maryanne offered a bubbly greeting as she pushed past Elle and me and made a bee-line for Maddie's room. Moments later I was rushed by little Maddie, still in her pajamas. She hugged me around my middle and as I hugged her back I gazed out at our entire tribe gathered on the front lawn. The looks on everyone's faces were a mix of smiles and sadness. They had accepted us, and notably me, into their lives and shared what little they had with us as if we had been friends and family forever, and now... we were leaving. From the back of the small group, Jimmy spoke up.

"Been saving these... for something." He began. "D-d-d-didn't know what for 'til yesterday, but anyhow... these are for you." He proudly displayed two nearly pristine mountain bikes.

"For us?" Elle called out over my shoulder with excitement. "That's gonna be a huge help. Thank you all so much for everything you have done for us."

It was an emotional morning. The hugs and handshakes were abundant and we felt like we were saying good-bye forever. There was a part of me that believed we might be. We donned our backpacks and Elle slung her trusty rifle over her shoulder. When we were walking our new bicycles to the road, followed by our friends, Maddie ran up ahead of the rest to say one more farewell. I knelt down to give her a proper hug and when I squeezed her as tight as I could, her whisper let me know, we would meet again.

"Don't forget to look for me at the water... I'll be there waiting for you." She spoke with confidence and sincerity and at that moment... I knew.

"I won't leave the water until I find you," I whispered back and kissed her cheek.

Maddie turned to Elle and they embraced so long and so deeply, I didn't think that Elle could sense what I did, even when little Maddie whispered to her. "I can't wait to see you again... all of you."

Elle fought back her tears and softly said goodbye to the child. As we rode away slowly west, I could hear the voices calling out goodbye and farewell and one little voice above the rest shouted out a hopeful thought.

"See you next Genesis Day!" The girl's voice shouted out happily.

*****

With the wind at our backs, we rolled down the pavement for hours without stopping. There was no 'Tour de France' effort or speed in our ride. It began more casually. We stayed side by side mostly and even talked as the miles rolled by beneath us. The day faded into evening and we pulled our bikes off of the road and into a patch of woods where we made camp for the night. We missed our friends, the comforts of our own little house and most of all our 'adopted' daughter, Maddie. We talked through the evening about where we had been and where we might find ourselves in the months to come until our tongues and minds were tired enough for sleep.

Morning came, cold and bleak, and the unforgiving ground had left us more stiff and achy than when we had stopped to rest. A few hours of riding at a fair pace had relieved both the cold and the stiffness. Again, the day had passed noon and the sun raced away from us. As the distance between us and Barnhill grew, our longing to return grew as well, until something caught my attention.

"Look!" I yelled out to Elle who was slightly behind me. A green reflective sign just ahead on our right gave a new hope that we hadn't had in a very long time. The sign read: 'Independence City Limits / POP 784'.

The trees had grown up along the sides of the road, and snow-capped peaks towered in the distance beyond, but no sign of any city, town or even building could be seen. Even though I kept my morale up on the outside, deep down inside, I was expecting the worst possible outcome; the devastated remains of what was once a quaint mountain town, possibly overrun by Takers who were awaiting our arrival. The paved, two-lane highway had begun to slowly decline and the sound of spinning wheels hummed in our ears. Inertia and gravity took effect and before long, we were coasting at a dangerously fast speed and had to begin riding our brakes to keep from losing control. Elle's white knuckled grip eased up. Her heart pounded and the blood coursed through her veins. An extreme excitement whisked her away to a place with no fear or worry, no aliens and no struggle for survival. Speeding past me, the grin on her face gleamed and suddenly I caught a glimpse of who this amazing woman had been, who she could be and who I hoped she would someday be again.

The road steepened and carried on ahead for a quarter of mile or so before yellow warning signs alerted us to slow down for a sharp right-hand curve. Elle had gained almost a hundred yards on me and I watched as she flew down the smooth, dotted asphalt. Sitting up straight, she let go of the hand grips and stretched her arms out wide. I watched as she mentally transformed into a soaring eagle, independent, free and beautiful. Something quickly went wrong. Elle's hands shot back to the handlebars and the bike quivered and weaved uncontrollably as she squeezed the brakes forcefully. The front wheel cut quickly to her left and then back to the right. The speed and force that had carried her so effortlessly forward now was catapulting Elle over the front of the mountain bike and tossing the bicycle end over end, crashing into the pavement over and over again, before coming to a stop in the overgrown grass and weeds beyond the side of the road. Elle had tumbled as brutally as her bicycle and when she finally came to a stop, she was curled up tightly in a fetal position with one arm behind her back. I could hear her cries of pain over the roaring wind in my ears, which terrified me.

I tucked my head and sped down the hill towards the horrific scene of the crash. My mind raced faster than my bike, imagining how badly she could be hurt, and what of the child that she might be carrying? I managed to maintain my composure, sliding my bike to a halt sideways with one foot on the ground and then jumping off before it even came to a complete stop. I rushed over to Elle's whimpering mass that had always been a pillar of unwavering strength. I could feel my heart beating wildly in my chest, hear it in my ears and I was breathing as hard as if I had just finished running a marathon. That was the moment it hit me... that unmistakable scent... The air was heavy with the putrid smell of death and rotting flesh. This was not the smell of roadkill in the hot summer sun; this was far worse. I hesitated for but a moment when I instinctively put the thought and smell of death out of my mind. I hunkered down over Elle's shaking form when I knew this was bad, very bad. Her left arm seemed obviously broken, twisted and bent in the most unnatural way.

"Oh God!" I did not mean to say that out loud, but I could not take my words back. "Elle, are you okay?" Stupid question! I was such an idiot. "I mean, I know you aren't okay, but..." What the hell was I supposed to say? "Your arm looks like it's broken pretty badly, are you hurt anywhere else?"

Elle moaned and sobbed, but said nothing in response. If only I could reach into my pocket, take out my cell phone and call 911 and wait patiently for an ambulance to arrive. It was a fleeting thought and its only purpose was to cause frustration and point out how truly helpless we were. Again, the abhorrent smell of rot stung my nostrils, burning a memory into my mind that I would never forget. I knew that what I had to do would be excruciatingly agonizing for her, but I had no choice.

"Babe..." I spoke softly as if it would cause less pain. "Can you hear me?"

"Yeah." Her trembling lips squeaked out amidst her sobs of despair.

"I am going to do everything I can, but what I won't do is lie... this is probably gonna hurt like hell." I gritted my teeth and prepared to gently move her arm enough to unclasp the backpack strap and attempt to remove the wrecked rifle she was carrying.

Her arm lay limp and twisted behind her back, awkwardly poised across her backpack. I gingerly slid my right hand under her forearm and my left under her elbow. I held my breath as if I were going to feel the painful sensation that I was about to cause. With the care and stealth of a surgeon, I raised her arm and elbow in synchronicity and just when it was high enough to lift over her side, I felt it roll and twist on its own. With a popping sound, Elle's shoulder slipped back into the socket and she unleashed a hellish scream from the pain. I squeezed the sides of the shoulder strap clasp and it clicked loudly and the two halves of the strap shot apart and the pressure that it held against Elle's shoulder was released. She moaned in relief between her sobs and snotty sniffles. My next task was to remove the rifle strap, which was a simpler task since it had no bearing on her pain and injured arm.

I rifled through my backpack and dug out one of the only two t-shirts I had packed. Without hesitation, I ripped the shirt in such a way that I was able to make a crude sling for Elle's arm to rest in and I used the sleeve scraps to bandage her knee and a dampened one to wipe clean the road-rash on her cheek and forehead. In time, Elle was sitting up and I had removed her pack completely. While I waited for her to be ready to travel again, I assessed the damage to the bike.

"The rifle is a loss... barrel's bent. It's too dangerous to try to use now, and it wouldn't be accurate at all anymore. Oh... and you won't be going anywhere on this thing." I held up Elle's bike. Its front rim and forks were completely bent and twisted. "I suppose it got us this far, at least."

"I'm sorry." Her tone clued me into the fact that she was beating herself up for the accident. "When that stench hit me, I freaked... and that's when I lost control."

"I know, I've honestly been gagging since I first smelled it." Had there been much on my stomach, I probably would have lost it. "We can use my bike to hang the backpacks on, whenever you feel up to heading on to Independence."

"I'm as ready as I'm gonna get. I could sit in the middle of the road all day, but I don't think I'd ever feel much like moving anywhere, so..." She grunted and groaned and discovered, even more, abrasions and bruises when she found her feet.

I walked the mountain bike slowly while Elle limped noisily beside me. The road took a sharp turn just ahead, but with our pace, I was afraid we may never reach it, much less make it all the way to Independence, however far that may actually be. I had every hope of seeing a building or

79

steeple rising above the tree line but there was nothing. What seemed like an hour later, we finally rounded the sharp corner at the bottom of the hill. A breeze struck us hard with the mordacious stench of death once again, but our eyes were drawn to the distant sight of the edge of the tiny burg of Independence. Our hopes of finding a town that had been untouched by the Titans and Takers had sunk, but we did still believe that we might find some shelter and perhaps more vital supplies.

Trudging along, the malodor burned our noses and the promise of finding survivors was utterly eliminated. Scattered buildings and homes grew closer together as we made our way into the small settlement. There was something else scattered ahead. Small dark forms, like half-filled trash bags, dotted the pavement and roadsides before us. A horrifying realization hit us like a prizefighter's punch to the gut, taking all of the air and motivation from us. The garbage bag lumps we had seen from a distance had become the limp, desiccated and rotting corpses of the innocent townsfolk. The alien beings, Ahsusha, and Takers had indiscriminately taken the lives of men, women and children. From the sheer number of bodies, and the overwhelming odor, it would seem that perhaps none were taken, and the life's energy had been stripped from the entire town, but for what reason?

Like a train wreck that steals your attention and will not allow you to look away, we tried to hide our eyes from the death that surrounded us. Every decaying cadaver we passed filled us with dread and hopelessness. The death that surrounded us had been a distraction, but the further we ventured, the more I began to notice something that was absent... destruction. There were no fragments of houses or buildings, not even a broken window. Several homes and a visitors center were behind us, and a town square was just ahead. Silence filled the air, and we had even found ourselves unable to speak. The square was lined with buildings from the turn of the twentieth century that stretched the entire length of the block. A half a dozen varied storefronts gave each block the appearance of being many individual structures. The first store we passed was a bookstore. Its showcase window was lined with displays of the most popular bestsellers.

"Oh! I love that series!" Elle broke the silence. "Forever ASH was my favorite."

"Frost & Flame, huh?" I responded honestly. "Never heard of it."

"What about that one?" She pointed to the next array of books esthetically exhibited. "Stepping Stones... you've heard of that one, right?"

"Honestly?" I smiled and almost laughed. "Kinda have amnesia, but I don't think I was ever much of a reader."

"Whaaaat?" She said in a high pitched voice as if my statement was unacceptable.

"Seriously. I don't remember much, but I definitely don't remember reading any..." The rattling of an empty can came from somewhere behind us and cut me off mid-sentence. Elle and I stood as still as statues and after a second, I slowly turned my head to attempt to find the source of the sound. I spotted nothing, not even an aluminum soft drink can rolling down the street. We waited motionless and silent for a few minutes before carrying on to the next store, which was a salon, and then the next. The second shop had Elle drooling for a haircut and a 'mani-pedi' as she called it. The third store was vacant, but the fourth was a small town pharmacy. I quickly checked the anodized aluminum storefront door to find it unlocked. Elle and I darted inside and were surprised to find it in perfect order.

"Let's find you some pain meds first, and then we can stuff as much as we can in our packs." I excitedly said.

"I don't really need any pain killers, but we should get all of the antibiotics and stuff like that we can find," She argued though I could hear the discomfort in her voice.

"We'll get some anyways... just in case. And... vitamins, supplements, that kind of stuff. Might be good since I don't know when we'll see a fresh orange or anything." I thought it might be good to be able to get as many nutrients as we could, however, we could.

"Good idea... and prenatals, just in case, right?" She actually smiled as we pillaged through the pharmacy shelves.

"I found a real sling and some braces!" I shouted out from the back of the store to Elle who was behind the pharmacy counter, where the prescription medicines were kept. Before she could answer, the sound of the front door closing caused me to spin around, expecting a malicious intruder, but there was nothing... I saw no one.

Elle Leaned over the counter, poking her head around the corner. "What was that?"

"Not sure. Maybe the wind." I made a statement, but my tone posed it as more of a question.

"Maybe... it was a little windy, I guess." She tried to reassure me, but just as the words left her lips, we heard another shuffling sound from within the store.

"Who's there?" I called out and we both nervously awaited some response, but again... nothing.

"Okay, this is just creepy," Elle said just above a whisper. "You remember those books I was talking about?"

"Yeah..." I answered sarcastically. "I have a bit of amnesia, but I think I can remember what happened less than an hour ago.

"Well... do you believe in ghosts, because with all of the death here..." She began with a quiver in her words. "This whole town could be haunted."

"Are you serious?" I teased. "Do you really believe in that stuff?"

"It's possible!" She defended herself. "I mean seriously... a year ago I wouldn't have believed in aliens coming to Earth, and now..."

"Point..." I couldn't argue her reasoning, but before I could finish I heard the sound again. I leaned back to make eye contact with Elle and placed my finger to my lips in a silent 'shhh' signal. I crouched down and laid my head against the composite tiled floor. Unfortunately, the aisles of shelving went all the way to the floor and I could not see under them and across the room. I began to sneak across the floor slowly, cautiously peeking around each corner and down each aisle, wondering if I might be confronted by... a ghost.

Chapter 7

The Determined Dandelion

The sound of my hands, knees, and shoes making contact with the hard composite tile floor was only exceeded by the pounding of my heart and the imagined sound of Elle's breath. Creeping slowly, aisle to aisle, my pulse quickened with every empty aisle I passed, knowing I was about to face our intruder by process of elimination. My inner warrior struggled with my inner child. One voice in my head was telling me to prepare for my worst nightmare and death while the other was laughing, calling the other voice a scaredy-cat and saying I was about to come face to face with a raccoon or some other small vermin. The lack of sounds made me wonder if I would find anything at all, or if I had just discovered a new cardio workout that would make you sweat, breathe heavily and not even exert any effort.

Of course, I had passed every aisle and was down to the last one that was parallel with the entrance. The desire to suck in a deep breath was difficult to ignore, but I knew, now more than ever, silence was my ally. I was preparing for fight or flight. Scenarios played out in my mind, and I hoped that if needed Elle and I could quickly find and escape through the rear exit. It was just then that a thought crossed my mind... I had no weapon. I could only hope that 'fight' was not necessary. I collected myself and my thoughts and decided the best course of action was the element of shock and surprise, so I jumped to my feet and rushed around the corner into aisle one.

Elle hid silently behind the pharmacy counter, listening for my movements and any clues of what may be transpiring out of her view. The seconds ticked away slowly and she found herself glancing at the clock on the wall even though the hands were frozen at 5:14 and 43 seconds. Her nervous curiosity had her on edge and her fingers were anxiously fidgeting until she could not stand it any longer. Cautiously she rolled to one side and raised herself to her knees. Her fingers crept over the edge of the counter-top and she pulled her eyes just above the plane of the laminate top. Wide-eyed, she scanned the vacant scene. Just when she thought she should duck back into hiding, I jumped to my feet and raced around the last row of shelves, packed and cluttered with health and beauty aids.

"AAAAAAHHHHHHH!!" Waving my hands in the air, I jumped out into the open and vulnerable space of aisle one. My mouth hung open as I stood there in shock, with my arms raised high. Had an intruder with a gun wanted to kill me, I would have just given them the perfect opportunity and target. "Elle..." I looked back over my shoulder and tried to coerce my partner to come join me.

Elle's eyes were bugging and felt like they would pop out of their sockets. She watched over the counter and saw that my hands remained lifted overhead as if I were surrendering, or were being held at gunpoint, or perhaps, I was motionlessly trying to avoid frightening off some furry visitor. Deep down in her heart, she believed that I would not have called her name if I were in any danger. The rush of adrenaline caused her hands to shake as she lifted the hinged countertop and pushed through the swinging, spring-hinged half door. She gasped as the movement of the swinging door filled the shop with rhythmic squeaks and knocks. Hesitantly, she left the noisy door and stepped up behind me with her one good arm raised over her head as well.

Before us stood a young boy, ten or twelve years old at the most, holding a can of soup in one hand, poised to hurl it like a projectile weapon. He was not very tall, but for his height, he was thin and lanky. Odd and unnatural would have been the best way to describe him. He was dressed in blue jeans and a plain red t-shirt. His hair was blonde and wispy and a pair of oversized sunglasses adorned his pasty, white face. Only an inch long, his fine and nearly white hair stood on end all over his head, giving him the appearance of a walking dandelion.

"We don't want to hurt you," I said calmly, not wanting to frighten him. "My name is Tanner. What's yours?"

"Hey lady, is he telling the truth?" His voice cracked like an adolescent though he looked too young to be going through the awkward change into manhood.

"Yep... we were just looking for some medicine..." She cocked her head to the side, motioning to her lame arm. "I had a bike wreck and hurt my arm pretty bad."

"I had a bike wreck last year." He seemed comfortable talking to Elle. "I got pretty bruised up and banged my head pretty hard, but I'm okay now, I guess."

"So, would it be okay if we put our arms down?" Elle asked politely.

"Yeah... I guess so." The cotton topped boy squeaked out the words and shrugged his shoulders. "I knew you weren't going to hurt me anyways..."

"Oh, you did?" I smiled. "Then you are braver and smarter than I am... I wasn't sure if you were gonna hurt us or not." I teased, hoping to make him feel more in control.

"Yeah, I knew." He reiterated. "Cause your kinda like me." He removed his sunglasses and I immediately recognized his eyes, and how they mirrored mine.

"They couldn't get you either, huh?" I gave him a wink, which brought a crooked smile to his face.

"So where are the others?" Elle asked from behind me.

"Others?" He echoed her word hollowly.

"Yeah, you know... the other town's people." She clarified her question.

"They're all over the place." He crinkled his nose. "And they started to smell really bad, but it's getting better now, I think."

"We noticed, but what I think Elle meant was... where are the other survivors, like people you are staying with?" I was taken aback by his nonchalant remarks about the rotting corpses that were strewn across the town.

"I guess you mean my dad and my sister, back at home... that's who I *stay* with." His face showed no emotion as he spoke. "I can take you there if you want."

"That would be great. Thanks." Elle said in such a quiet and kind voice that I almost didn't recognize it.

"We can come back and get some more stuff later," I said to Elle and took her by the hand. She nodded and I lead her out into the street behind the cotton topped boy, who still had not told us his name.

We strolled down the street silently, past the decaying and desiccated bodies of people that our young companion very likely knew. He turned back to us and smiled, saying, "I'm glad you're here. I've been waiting for you for a while."

After walking a few blocks and passing a small grocery store, a post office, a touristy gift shop called 'Mountain Memories' and someplace called *The 2nd*, we turned a corner towards the white-capped mountains that seemed to hang from the clouded sky. The narrow lane rose uphill and after only a hundred yards or so, we were headed out of 'town' and back into a woodsy area.

"Our house is just a little ways up there." He pointed ahead and the country twang was more apparent when he spoke this time.

"You never did tell us your name... You know my name is Elle and that's Tanner, and if you don't tell me your name, I'm gonna start calling you Dan... short for Dandelion." Elle sped up next to the young man.

"It's Daniel if you must know." He crossed his arms in a huff as if he were wanting to keep his identity a secret for some reason.

"Oh cool!" Elle exclaimed. "Like Daniel in the Lion's Den. Daniel... lions... get it? Daniel-lions?"

"Yeah, that is kinda cool, I guess." He halfheartedly smiled again.

I followed behind as we plodded up the hill and thought of how well Elle was at building friendships and trust with complete strangers. There was another thought that was stuck in the forefront of my mind; why was this boy, like me, unconquerable? The whites of his eyes having gone gray, and his pupils being a faintly glowing green must have been a very disturbing thing for him to have seen in a mirror. I can't say that I blamed him for wearing the sunglasses... Honestly, I was a bit envious and thought that I may have to find a pair for myself.

"There it is." Daniel pointed to a small, rustic, wood sided house. It was not run-down by any sense of the phrase, but it was not pristine either and showed its age in painfully obvious ways. Its architecture dated it to the 1960's or 70's. Though it was well taken care of, there were no replacement windows and the shingles on the roof were nearing the end of their life and had patches of green on the northern edges where moss was making itself a home. Tarnished aluminum framed the front door (which was probably original) and at some point in the distant past held a storm door. A small covered porch housed two chairs, crafted from four or five-inch thick tree limbs, and a large diameter log had been made into a very 'hillbilly' table between the two.

The daylight was dimming and the air was growing cool when Daniel reached for the doorknob. He gave it a turn without needing to unlock it.

"Come on in." He said as he pushed the door open and before I even entered the boy's home I understood his demeanor. A smile is sometimes a window to let our light shine out into the world. Other times it is a mask that hides the darkness within us. I took Elle's hand and squeezed it hard.

Leaning into her, I whispered quietly through her tangled hair. "Keep your composure, babe."

She nodded, understanding my words completely, bit her lip and shut her eyes tight while she put her mind into a calm and collected place. Passing the threshold, I pulled Elle into the house behind me by the hand. The dim light of sunset filtered in through the mismatched curtains. The foul odor and the dank interior lighting gave the young man's home the eerie feel of a horrific thriller film about a serial killer. I glanced around the room and heard Elle's near silent gasp when my eyes fixed on the source of the stench.

"That's ma dad." Daniel said casually as he walked past a well-worn recliner that held his father. "My sis is in her room back there." He pointed down a dark and narrow hallway. "Seems kinda weird to have people here that talk and stuff."

The man in the recliner rested with his feet propped up and his arms crossed in his lap. Positioned directly across from a rather small television, he held the remote control in his left hand. It was odd that he would be there even though there was no power, and therefore, no television... but the oddest and most disturbing thing was the man's state. His hair was matted, his skin was discolored and leathery looking and his lips were drawn back, exposing his yellowed teeth. Daniel's father's eyes were sunken deep as were his cheeks. This man, who Daniel had so nonchalantly introduced, was for lack of a better word... dead.

"Daniel..." Elle's voice trembled.

"Yeah?" He responded just before exiting into the next room.

"How did your dad... die?" She wondered how he had died in his easy chair. Had he simply sat there when the Ahsusha came and not put up a fight? Why hadn't he tried to run?

"Just like everybody else. The gray people came..." His eyes glazed over as he pulled the story from deep in his memory. "There were so many of them. A lot more than there were of us. They just grabbed people wherever they were and just sucked the life out of them, I guess. They tried to kill me too. I didn't fight, though."

"Why not?" The boy had peaked my curiosity. "Why didn't you run and hide?"

"I been fighting my whole life." He said solemnly. "I been real sick and I was just ready for it to all be over. When I saw my dad out there in the road, I just went out and stood there until they came for me, but it didn't work."

"Whadya mean, *it didn't work*?" Elle asked the question that was burning in my mind too though I was fairly certain I knew and even understood the answer he was about to give us.

"Well... they didn't come for me. I had to go find them." He caught me off guard. "I found a bunch of them going through town and I hollered out at 'em. When they finally took me to one of the glowy-eye people, he grabbed me and then kinda freaked out. He didn't kill me like I thought... I guess I killed him. That's when I started feeling better... and I guess that's when my hair started growing again. I haven't had any hair for a long time."

It was just then that I had another flash of memory from a life that seemed to belong to someone else. I remembered sitting next to my wife on the plane again. Sunlight was streaming in through the open windows and she held my hand tight. There was an intense pain deep in my head that radiated outward and I thought I would not be able to bear it.

"Maybe this doctor will be able to help..." She must have known of my pain. "He's supposed to be the best, right?" She raised the back of my hand to her face and pressed her lips to it gently. "Why don't you try to get some sleep? It's a long flight and I'll wake you before we land."

I snapped back quickly to the present, as the memory faded. "It was cancer, wasn't it... that made you lose your hair?" I blurted out without considering that it may have been a very touchy subject for our new young friend.

"Nope." He answered swiftly. "It was the medicine stuff. They told me the chemo would make my hair fall out and make me sick, but they didn't say I'd be that sick... I just didn't want to be sick anymore."

"Did you have to go someplace far away to see the doctor? Like, did you have to fly someplace?" I thought I was about to make a connection, but Elle looked at me strangely, like I had three glowing eyes (not two).

"Uh huh... we had to drive for like a couple of hours to get there," Daniel recalled. "Sometimes it took a little longer if there was traffic in the city."

"That means we are only a hundred miles or so from a good sized city, right?" I turned to Elle and spoke. "Maybe there are people there; maybe there are survivors..."

"Or maybe the Titans haven't even gone there." Elle finished my thought. "But sixty miles is a long damn walk."

"We've done twenty, we can do a hundred." I felt optimistic. "Plus, we can get plenty of supplies and we have Danny to help carry stuff."

"Why not just drive?" Daniel asked innocently.

"Well, I guess it's like this." I hadn't thought about someone his age not understanding the lack of power being sort of universal. "Just like there is no electricity; batteries, like the ones in cars, don't seem to work either."

96

Daniel closed his eyes tight, as if deep in thought. "While that may be true, due to the advanced EMP weaponry of the alien invaders, there are certain vehicles, such as those with a standard transmission, that can be started even without a battery."

"True..." I wondered how in the hell a boy this age understood so much that I hadn't even thought of. "I suppose it is possible."

"What's an EMP weapon?" Elle was, once again, thinking the same thing I was.

"An Electro-Magnetic-Pulse weapon." Daniel rubbed his finger under his nose to relieve an itch and opened his eyes slowly. "The military has EMP weapons, but they aren't very advanced. The alien people's pulse weapon might be different than ours. We lost all our power about a day before they even showed up."

"It's worth a shot. If we can't get a car to work, we won't be any worse off than we are now, plus we could take a lot more supplies in a car." I shrugged my shoulders, feeling 'one-upped' by a twelve-year-old.

"Why don't we try to find a car we can try this on, and then gather up whatever we can find..." Elle was being logical, and proactive. "...like guns."

Her idea made perfect sense. Why waste time packing more than we could carry if the car idea turned out to be a bust? The sun had dipped behind the horizon and the night sky grew dark quickly. The three of us set out in hopes of finding transportation and I knew our odds were slim, but we had to try.

"Hey Daniel..." I got the boy's attention as we walked. "Do you know anyone with an old hot rod kind of car, sports car, or anything like that?"

"Sure." He thought. "Mr. Burton has a few old cars. His house isn't far."

Chapter 8

Hitching a Ride

The sky was clear and dotted with a million pinpoints of starlight. The moon was growing fuller by the night and tonight it shed a faint glow on the world beneath it. Dew on the cool grass sparkled like a sea of diamonds beside the road we traveled down. Daniel pointed to his right and began to cut across the unruly and unkempt, grassy field, sparsely dotted with the growth of young trees. Elle and I followed the lad, and trusted in our youthful guide, across the field, through a patch of woods and eventually out onto a newly paved lane. It seemed apparent that Daniel, like me, could see quite well in the most minimal amount of light. Elle, on the other hand, relied on her survival skills and instincts to keep up with us.

"That's his place there." Daniel motioned towards a very nice, two story modern home. "My dad used to help him with odd jobs to make extra money."

"That's a cool house." I admired the obviously extravagant architecture. "Does he keep his cars in the garage, I guess?"

"Some of them. He has a lot of cars." Daniel explained. "He keeps some out back in the barn too."

We check the exterior of the home and found the back door unlocked. Once again, we trusted in our newly found friend to guide us through the house and to the garage. I paid little attention to the interior of the home and was only interested in finding out if our theory on the cars would work as we hoped. Daniel made a quick bee-line for the garage door and we filed into the two and a half car garage to find a nearly brand new, black, GMC, SUV and an almost new, silver, four-door, import sedan. Neither of these would serve our needs as they were both automatic transmission and couldn't be 'push started'.

"Well, I guess we check the barn then, huh?" Elle asked.

"Yeah, but first we need these." He opened a small, plastic box that was mounted on the wall and revealed several sets of marked keys, hung on hooks inside.

I scoured through the keys and found a set marked 'VW'. "This might just work."

Retracing our path, I lead the way out of Mr. Burton's house. Across the open yard stood an old barn. It was not one of the new styled, metal sided, pole barns. This barn had the look of one built a hundred years ago; wood sided, faded red in places, but mostly weathered and gray, with eroded edges that left open spaces between the side boards. The main door was large and made with the typical 'X' pattern bracing. Rollers mounted on the top fit into a rusty track and allowed the door to be opened by pushing hard against the crude, wooden handle. Leaning in with all of my weight and strength, the rollers creaked and the door slid to the side. The musty smell of damp and moldy hay crept out of the structure and for a moment, I had a memory of being on a relative's farm as a child, but the recollection quickly escaped me and I was brought back to the present.

"Is it in there?" Elle asked, being unable to see through the blackness of shadows.

"Maybe..." I answered, unsure of the truth.

"Here... I think this might help." Daniel rushed into the barn and snatched up a propane lantern that hung on the wall near the door. Twisting the valve, the gas hissed as it began to escape the canister. Picking up a lighter that rested on a cross-brace next to the lantern, Daniel gave a quick flick of the flint wheel. A halo of pale light surrounded the lantern and the boy. Like a sigh in reverse, Elle gasped. The sight before us looked much like a family of giant sleeping bears, deep in hibernation. Several huge forms filled the otherwise open space and cast dancing shadows on the walls as young Daniel moved into the center of the masses. Large, mildew and water stained canvases covered five uniquely shaped objects. Reaching the first canvas, I whipped it back onto itself, revealing a shiny silver quarter panel and hood.

"Is that a DeLorean?" Elle blurted out.

"Yep... that it is," I answered back.

"He was always workin' on this one. I never even saw him drive it." Daniel said, disappointingly.

"That's okay... there isn't enough room for three of us and no room to pack very much. I wouldn't want to take the DeLorean unless we could use it to go back in time before the Titans showed up." I made a poorly received joke about a popular 1980's film series. "I'm hoping one of these is an old VW beetle."

Looking over the remaining four covered vehicles, two were large boxy shapes, one was small and wedge shaped, but only one was slightly rounded and shaped similar to a beetle. Daniel held the lantern high while Elle and I took opposite corners of the tarp and, pulling it back, revealed the auto beneath.

"Cool! I've never seen that one before." Daniel exclaimed. "Why is that out here in the barn?"

"Good question." My heart sank when it hit me that the car I was certain would be a VW Beetle was actually a Mini-Cooper, and not even an old one. "Well, I guess we can see what these others are. Maybe one of them will work for us." I stood wallowing in my disappointment when I heard Elle's voice call out from behind me.

"Whoa!" She said. "Hey... Tanner? Check this out."

There was only one wheel exposed, but I immediately knew what I was looking at. The open wheel design, narrow front tires, and a fire-engine red tube frame were dead giveaways that Elle was about to uncover an 'open air' sand rail... more commonly known as a dune buggy. As she drew the tarp back, I knew without a doubt that this was the 'VW' that I was looking for. This was mechanical engineering at its finest, yet simplest, form. There were no high-tech gadgetry or computer sensors to be disabled by the EMP of the Titans. The only 'brain' this buggy had, was the one that sat in the driver's seat.

"Yes!" I literally screamed out, in what was possibly the loudest voice I had used since my night calling out in the desert. "This is almost as perfect as a beetle would have been."

"Almost?" Daniel questioned me.

"Well... I doubt it has much luggage room, and it's probably a two-seater." I knew that this would make our reaching the next destination in a timely manner even more important and it also meant that Daniel would have to ride on Elle's lap. It wasn't the safest idea, but I doubted we would come across much traffic.

"True," Elle said as she rolled back the tarp revealing the rest of the rail buggy. "I don't see why we couldn't strap some suitcases or something to the top. I mean... if the city isn't totally destroyed, and it's only an hour away, we shouldn't need much. Besides, if this thing actually works, we could always drive back if we need to." Elle thought for a minute. "You *do* know how to drive a stick shift, right?"

I withdrew the keys from my front pocket with a smile and climbed into the driver's seat. The key slipped effortlessly into the ignition and with a quick twist... nothing; not even a click. Releasing the parking brake, I popped the shifter out of gear and jumped back out of the iron framed beast. I leaned against the windshield frame and grasped the steering wheel in my right hand. I grunted out loud and with a little effort, the buggy began to roll forwards toward the open sliding door. Elle joined me on the opposite side of the buggy and together, guided by Daniel's lantern light, we rolled the open vehicle out into the cool air of the night.

"Okay, we have to get up some decent speed to get this to work," I explained. "Over that way." I pointed to the left, where the back yard had a slight downhill slope. I cut the steering wheel in that direction and we rolled the buggy into place.

"Daniel!" I called out to the boy in the old barn. "We're going to need your help too!" Elle and I remained in place and after setting the lantern on the ground, Daniel ran up to the back of the buggy and placed his hands around the welded cage that surrounded the chrome-encrusted, rotary engine. "After I jump in, you two need to keep pushing... on three, okay?...One... Two... THREE!"

I screamed out the last number and it only took a few steps before the dune buggy was rolling freely and we were jogging along with it at a swift pace. I jumped through the open frame and into the driver's seat. My heart pounded as I straightened my left leg and engaged the clutch. We were continuing to gain speed when I slipped the shifter into first gear with a slight pop. Daniel and Elle were at a dead run when I popped the clutch. A clunking repetitive sound ensued and I depressed the clutch again and goosed the gas pedal. With a pop-pop-pop-pop that continued to repeat itself, the low-tech motor growled and grumbled to life. I pulled the shifter knob straight down and into second gear. Easing out on the clutch, I gave the accelerator a hard punch, causing the light dune buggy to spin sideways, throwing grass and dirt into the air.

"Woooo!" I screamed out with exhilaration. Letting the car come to a resting stop out of gear, I pulled the parking break into action. There were only three switches on the flat, painted metal, dashboard. Flipping the first toggle, a row of lights across the top of the rail buggy came on and turned the darkness to daylight. The vibration of the running motor and the rumbling sound of the racing style header thrilled me far beyond what it should have. I quickly turned the lights out again and stepped out of the car, leaving it running to hopefully recharge the battery.

"Do we pack up and go now, or wait until tomorrow?" I put the question to a vote.

"Now!" Daniel popped off quickly. "I don't want to be here anymore."

"Sounds fine to me, but we do need to pack up some things first." Elle sympathetically agreed with the distraught pre-teen. "We might be able to find most of what we need here... especially if he has any guns."

"Sure he does," Daniel said as if it were common knowledge. "Everybody's got guns."

"Okay, looks like we have a little quest for supplies. Let's get what we need and get on our way as soon as we can." I switched off the motor and slid the keys safely into my pocket as if there might actually be someone who might steal our transportation. "We'll meet back here in fifteen minutes."

Back inside the house, I sent Daniel to the kitchen to gather up some easy to eat foodstuffs and anything he could find to drink. Elle was put to the task of gathering up first aid items, pain relievers in particular. I, on the other hand, searched the house for weapons. It was in the finished basement living room that I found what I was looking for... sort of. In the corner of the rustic, 'Early American' decorated room stood a large gun safe. There was a dial and a keyhole. I hoped that the key or the combination to the lock would be easily found. I scoured the house, tearing apart drawers and searching corners until it came to me and I checked under the mattress in the master bedroom. It was a bit surprising to find that Mr. Burton not only hid the key between his mattress and box-springs but also the combination to the gun safe. I took both down to the safe, nervously unlocked it, and hoped I would find what I was looking for. I was not disappointed.

By the time I made it back to the rail buggy, Elle and Daniel were already there. In fact, they had been there long enough that Daniel had two large carry bags, stuffed with various food items, poised on the sheet metal roof of the dune buggy. As I walked across the dewy lawn, Elle reappeared from the barn with a lantern in hand and a length of rope over the shoulder of her good arm.

"We can tie the bags down with this." She explained as she sat the lantern on the ground.

"I was thinking about you being a 'one armed bandit', so I brought you this." I slid a nylon strap from my shoulder and presented Elle with a shoulder holster that held a nearly unused 9mm pistol, made with three sleek and convenient, Velcro pockets that held full seven round clips.

"Oh, my..." Elle grinned as I placed the holster over her bad shoulder so that she could reach the 9mm with her good hand and fastened it snugly. Being so close, Elle was unable to resist a small kiss. "I really do love you, ya know?" Her stomach fluttered as she spoke the words.

"Yeah, I know," I said sarcastically through my embarrassment, which was answered by a well-deserved shove. "Hey 'Big D', do you think there is room in one of those bags for this?" I held up a small bag that I had crammed full of ammunition. "And our backpacks too?"

"Sure. That won't take up much room." He said, taking the small, yet heavy, bag from my hand, and climbing on top of the buggy, he crammed it into one of the zippered bags. I handed up both backpacks that I had been toting since the tragic bicycle wreck, and he made short work of wedging them tightly between the two new packed bags.

"Looks to me like we are headed on a cross-country trip, not a couple of hours away." I teased, but I knew that anything could happen... things had a way of going wrong.

While the young man was on top of our transport, I tossed up the rope and with a little direction, he snaked it through the handles and I wrapped it around the open metal roof several times and cinched it down tightly with a knot that came from someplace deep in my memory. Like Elle, I also had a 9mm pistol neatly tucked into a holster under my left arm. I helped Daniel down from the car-top and Elle and I took our places in the two bucket seats of the dune buggy. Daniel reluctantly took a seat on Elle's lap and she stretched the seatbelt around them, locking it in place with a metallic click. Releasing the parking brake, I found the sweet spot between the clutch and gas pedals and we began to roll forward. I clicked on the headlight toggle switch and our adventure was on again.

Reaching the paved road, I eased into second gear and we rolled along at what seemed like lightning speed. It was actually only about fifteen miles an hour when I shifted into third gear and idled along around twenty for a while as we cruised through town, avoiding the resident bodies that were occasionally scattered about on the road. For a moment, my mind drifted to what felt like a distant world, another life... and to Maddie. I wondered how she was, what the Barnhill tribe was up to, and how long it might be before we met up again. I was brought back to reality when Elle broke the silence.

"Does anyone know where we are going?" Her question made a valid point. Did Daniel know the way to the city, and if so, could we rely on a twelve-year-old to guide us once again?

"It's easy..." Daniel stated. "Just turn right, up here at the highway and follow it to highway 58. Turn right again and Bakersfield is only another hour farther."

"Who needs a GPS, when you've got a 'Big D' navigation service?" Elle stroked the young man's ego and brought a genuine smile to his otherwise expressionless face.

We drove on through the night with the wind in our hair, and though it was uncomfortably cold, the moving air was a refreshing change. It was an obvious change, but it was not the only one. The season had changed from summer to autumn; Like Daniel, I had changed from who I once was, to who I had become, and not just as a person, but from a person into this odd hybrid of human and alien; Elle had changed from an average young woman to a fearless warrior and survivalist and then changed again to a brave, young, mother-to-be... but there was more. There was a feeling of change in the air that I could not yet understand.

My mind wandered as the miles slipped by and before I knew it, I was taking the I-58 exit. In the thick of autumn, the cold, mountain air stung our cheeks and fingers and chilled our watery eyes. I drove relatively slow compared to the speed limit, but the openness of the dune buggy and the bitter cold air made our 35 mph speed seem exponentially faster. Our trio remained silent. Perhaps the others were enjoying the swiftness of our journey and remembering how life was before the Titans came... or perhaps they, like myself, wondered what we would find when we reached a real city.

There was the possibility that it had remained untouched by the invasion; that the Titans and Takers had not yet reached this city. There was another possibility that I dreaded. It was entirely possible that we would know the fate of Bakersfield long before we reached it by its stench alone. The streets, buildings, and houses might be strewn with hundreds of thousands of rotting corpses. The city and suburbs might be overrun with Takers, a quarter of a million or more, led by Ahsusha, bent on world domination. Though I seemed to have some useful powers of persuasion and the ability to blend in with them, I dared not think of confronting the obedient 'alien zombies' in such overwhelming numbers. Daniel might find himself accepted by the Ahsusha much like I was, but Elle, on the other hand, would attract them like a magnet. Her individuality, her humanity, would be sought out and they would not stop until they had taken her.

The hours flew by and I saw the darkened city skyline, against the starlit sky, in the distance. It was growing late, possibly eleven o'clock, or even midnight, but I did not see a single light, which caused my hopes to sink. I watched the informational signs as we neared Bakersfield. I downshifted and slowed to a creeping 15mph when I saw the city limits sign. We created our own wind, so I was unable to determine the direction of the natural movement of the air; however, I did not notice any lingering odor, certainly not the reeking smell of death from a hundred thousand corpses or more. Though my feelings of what I expected to find were mixed and confusing, I did believe it would be best to find shelter for the rest of the night and embark on our search of the city at dawn.

"Look for a side road, driveway, or anything that might lead to a house," I spoke loudly, over the rumble of the motor and the low roar of the passing winds.

"We just passed one." Daniel quickly responded, pointing behind us.

"Go back?" Elle posed the choices. "...or look for the next one?"

I could sense the uneasiness in her voice. "Back." I decided it was best. We had encountered no Taker, Ahsusha, or person along the highway, but I could not say what perils may lie ahead. "Hang on!" I shouted as I swung wide to the right and then cut the steering wheel hard to the left. The dune buggy had such a short wheelbase that we made a very tight U-turn and the supplies that we had strapped to the roof of the car shifted, as did Elle and Daniel. Their arms flailed about trying to find something to hold on to.

"Holy hell!" Elle scolded me. "Was that really necessary? You could have at least thought about using the brakes."

I thought of a sarcastic rebuttal, but instead, I shrugged my shoulders and decided that I would remain quiet. I searched the roadsides for the roadway that Daniel had spoken of. Only fifty yards back up the highway I spotted a narrow gravel lane that jutted off to the left and disappeared into the woods. This time, I slowed down considerably and inched our way off of the highway and onto the misty forest lane. Just where the road entered woods, a cable, strung between two wooden 4x4 posts, blocked our way. I popped the buggy out of gear and pulled the parking brake. Leaving the two strapped in their seats, I went to investigate.

"It's locked in place, and I don't think we can get around it, between the trees." I was uncharacteristically pessimistic.

"Let me out," Daniel said to Elle, who unlatched the seatbelt with a click and he leapt from the car like a wild animal released from a cage.

"Hmmm..." He studied the barricade closely. "Too bad we don't have a screwdriver." He mumbled to himself, and without another word, he began to twist at the threaded eye-bold that connected the cable to the wooden post. The more he unscrewed it, the tighter the cable became as it twisted back on itself. When it was just over half way removed, it became too difficult to turn any further. "Well, screw it!" He said loudly and grabbed the eye-bolt in hand and with a jerky tug and flying splinters, ripped it from its hold.

"Outdone by a twelve-year-old." I muttered under my breath, though apparently not quietly enough.

"Thirteen." Daniel corrected me with a snap, which pulled a boisterous laugh from Elle.

"Okay... I get it." I had given up before I had even tried. "Thanks, Daniel. Now, let's see where this road takes us."

Back in the open buggy, we slowly crept up the gravel lane into the forest. I flipped the toggle to turn the lights off, but at this pace, I could see well enough to safely navigate the narrow drive. Winding through the dense woods and gradually climbing upwards, our narrow path became more and more steep until it abruptly leveled off and opened up to nearly an acre of what appeared to be a camping area with only one structure. The narrow lane made an oval around the clearing with perpendicular parking spots radiating out like the rays of sunshine on a child's crayon drawing. A very large and rustic log cabin stood at the onset of the oval drive.

"Well, this looks like a bust," Daniel said with disappointment.

"Not necessarily," I reassured him. "Considering our current situation, if we can get inside, this should be just fine for a one night stay."

"Let's find a way in." Elle's lip quivered as she spoke and she desperately wanted to vigorously rub the warmth back into her arms, but her injury and sling made it impossible.

While Elle and Daniel searched the perimeter of the cabin for a way in, I noticed a rack of firewood and filled my arms with pieces that ranged from tiny kindling to large ¼ split logs. When I had an armload so large that I could barely see over it, I went in search of my companions. As I rounded the corner to the rear of the cabin, I found Elle boosting Daniel up with her one good arm. They had found a rather tiny, unlocked window about seven feet from the ground. Daniel was thin for his age and height, which allowed him to just squeeze through the narrow opening.

"Whooooaaa!" Daniel called out and his cry was immediately followed by a loud 'thud' from within. "I'm okay."

"You sure?" Elle could tell that his words were less than convincing.

"Yeah," Daniel grumbled sounding like the wind had been knocked out of him.

"See if you can unlock the back door. Tanner and I will meet you there."

Daniel did not answer, but we could hear his rustling around and the sound of an opening door inside. The two of us walked the short distance to the back door, where Daniel was already waiting with the door wide open. Elle went first and I followed close behind, which turned out to be a bit of a mistake.

"Watch your..." was all that Elle was able to get out before I caught my foot on the overhanging step up at the door's threshold.

With a clambering crash, my armload of wood and I spilled into the cabin, taking Elle down with me. Her screeching cry alerted me to the fact that this was not a gentle and humorous tumble to the floor. She had fallen on her bad shoulder... and fallen hard. Her shaky, sobs filled the air and, over and over again, I reiterated my apologies. I scooped her up and rushed her into the front room of the cabin.

The cabin opened up into a great room with finished wooden walls and vaulted ceiling, supported and ordained with massive wooden beams. A large semi-circle of sofas and easy chairs faced a wall, to my right, which was filled with an oversized fireplace. Straight ahead of me was a wall of windows, which stretched from floor to ceiling and to my left, was a windowless wall with three, stained wooden, six-panel doors. Placing her gently on the sofa closest to the fireplace, I kissed her forehead and offered my apology once again.

"I'm so sorry." I brushed her hair from her face with my hand. "Try to relax and I'll get the pain meds."

Elle said nothing but nodded as she stared at the floor, refusing to make eye contact with me. I rushed past Daniel, who was picking up the scattered mess of wood from the floor. Running out to the dune buggy, the chill in the air reminded me that fall was fading and winter would creep up on us as quickly as fall had. I snatched up a bottle of pain medicine and a one-liter bottle of water that Daniel had packed. It took only a few minutes to find the items, but by the time I had done so and was headed back to the cabin, a familiar scent filled my senses... the aromatic smoke of a campfire. When I re-entered the great room, I found Daniel kneeling in front of the large fireplace, and a small crackling fire growing just beyond its hearth. The sight before me stopped me in my tracks. A teepee of kindling had been lit and it's orangey-yellow glow filled that side of the room with a warmth and feeling of hope and home. The silhouette of the boy outlined against the growing flames, and the way the dancing light highlighted Elle's form as she rested on the sofa and accentuated the very sensual lines of her figure, had a mystical magic about it.

Coming to my senses, I brought the water and painkillers to Elle. I opened the water bottle and sat it on the floor in front of her. Unlocking the child-safety lid, I shook out two pills and handed them to her. Popping them in her mouth, she picked up the water and washed them down with an audible gulp. Daniel stoked the fire and added a larger piece of oak to the now glowing embers. I replaced the cap on the water bottle and the lid on the prescription pain medicine and took a seat on the floor near Elle.

"I don't mean to be a big baby, but this hurts more than when I broke my arm as a kid." She needlessly apologized. "I wish I could heal like you do."

"I wish that too," I smiled and caressed the side of her face.

"You can, ya know?" Daniel muttered over his shoulder, still focusing his attention on growing the fire.

"What do you mean?" I asked as if I had no clue of what he was talking about, but a memory snapped to mind; Maddie.

"Everyone has the potential; it's kind of supposed to be that way... that was supposed to be the plan," Daniel spoke with an understanding that was beyond his years. "Well, to be fair, it was one of the plans."

"You have my attention." I coaxed him to continue.

"Mine too." Elle perked up and propped her head up on her good arm.

"There are two plans, really. The first was set in place by the leader of a race that has no name that can be spoken, so I just think of them as 'The Aliens'. This leader's plan was to come to earth with some of the hand-picked, elite aliens. They wanted to inhabit human bodies so they could reproduce. The rest of the human race would be used as a source of energy... sort of like food until they were almost used up. Then they would just be servants and their only purpose would be to do physical work and reproduce... more food." Daniel paused. "Can I have a drink?"

"Of course." I handed him the water bottle, so fascinated that I was unable to say anything else.

"Well, that was plan one, in a nutshell." He took a drink and swallowed hard. "Ahhh..." He sighed as he exhaled. "Thanks. There was one of 'The Aliens', one of the leaders, who wanted the ability to reproduce also, but *he*, for lack of a better word, wanted to find a peaceful way to do it. This leader was commander of one of the giant crafts and came to earth to try to warn us. *He* had something that the others had evolved away from... *he* had emotion. I think plan number two was to create an awareness and a resistance by getting here ahead of the invasion and making us all part alien, or something like that... but *he* didn't get to."

"Emotions..." I thought out loud. "It seemed like emotions confuse the Titans. It may even make them shut down completely, like an

116

overload. I'm starting to think that the more emotions that are present, the less the path of the Titan is certain. And I know this is going to sound... I dunno... dumb? But I think maybe the Titans color have something to do with the emotions that are present, or maybe it has to do with how closely they are following the true objective."

"So, they are fighting amongst themselves too?" Elle asked curiously.

"I think so..." Daniel was an amazing wealth of knowledge, but he was also a typical thirteen-year-old. "I wanna drive one of those Titans. I think I could. That would be so cool!"

"I've 'driven' one, and yeah... it was pretty damn cool," I smiled at the young man and he returned a very toothy grin. "You know, something that seemed very queer to me was that the Titan I was on was dark blue, but when it crashed into the ravine, it was chalky white colored. I think it was because I was thinking of you." I turned my smile towards Elle.

"But how do you know all of this stuff?" Elle was confused.

"Well, I guess after the alien thing didn't kill me, my head was full of a lot of stuff that wasn't there before." He began to explain.

"Mine too!" I remembered the overwhelming feeling of being bombarded with ideas and images and information. "...but I don't know if I got the same info you did. This is all kinda new to me."

"Really?" He seemed surprised.

"Yeah... my brain had so much going on inside of it I thought it would explode, but I couldn't really get much out of it." I felt suddenly inferior to a thirteen-year-old... again.

"It took me a couple of weeks to figure out what I know, and I think I've just scratched the surface, ya know?" He ran his fingers through his dandelion hair. "I didn't have much else to do, but sit there alone and think."

"That makes sense. I had a feeling I could get a lot of information out of my head too, if I could just concentrate on it hard enough, without any distractions." I wondered what had been implanted in my brain. "I think we should get a little rest before we end up sitting here talking until the sun comes up. It would be good to get an early start tomorrow."

"You're right." Elle agreed. "Those pain killers have me kind of loopy anyway. I'm about to fall asleep already."

"Okay, if we have to." Daniel wanted to stay up and talk, and frankly, so did I, but I knew we needed sleep.

We would hopefully have a chance to talk in the near future though nothing was definite. While Daniel stoked up the fire one last time and found the fireplace screen, I searched through the other rooms and found a closet with a few pillows and blankets. It was mere minutes, but by the time I returned Elle was fast asleep and snoring softly. I handed one pillow and a team logoed, fleece throw to Daniel and then gingerly raised Elle's head to slide a pillow under her. I draped a beautifully patterned quilt over her and took the last blanket to a nearby recliner. I soon dozed off with thoughts of how much had changed since Elle had found me in the desert. When this had all started, everyone was afraid of having a fire, especially at night, but now, I thought, I could almost sense when the aliens were near. Months had passed since then, we had made new friends and lost many of them, and we had both changed in our own ways.

Chapter 9

The Specialist

The tip of my nose was chilled and the subtle sounds of rustling outside of the cabin caught my attention as I came to consciousness. In the predawn hours, the oversized great room had grown cold. Avoiding any real movement, I pried one eye half open and glanced around the room. By the hazy, dim light that drifted in through the windows, I could tell it was still very early in the morning. Elle and Daniel were fast asleep on their respective sofas. More rustling noises came from just outside the window and I opened both eyes and blinked hard to shake off the sleep and focus.

Two young deer were wandering through the campground and had stopped just outside of one of the large, foggy, picture windows to nibble on the short grasses. I found comfort in watching them as they continued about with their natural and instinctive actions. It was good to know that *everything* hadn't changed.

The movement of the lowering footrest on the recliner caught the attention of everyone. Elle and Daniel stirred groggily while the eyes and ears of the yearlings perked up and the nearest one looked directly into my dimly lit eyes. White billowing steam shot from its nose with a snort, and the two turned and sprang away and bounced into the dense woods in a few short bounds... and just like that, they were gone. I kept the images and encounter to myself as the three of us gathered ourselves and prepared to say good-bye to our short lived shelter. Before my companions and I were fully awake, we were climbing into the dew drenched buggy once again.

I produced the key and placed it in the ignition before strapping myself in. Biting my lip, depressing the clutch and tapping the gas pedal, I said a silent prayer and turned the key. The starter turned sluggishly, and even though I was expecting to have to unbuckle and push start the car again, the motor caught and grumbled to a start. Daniel raised his hands and Elle made a fist and pumped her one good arm in the air, expressing our little victory. Life was really about the little victories. Not everyone becomes hugely successful; not everyone is rich; those who want for nothing are few and far between... the truth is that nearly everyone (probably everyone) would be sorely disappointed if they relied on a huge success for happiness. We had a battle ahead of us, maybe even a war, but finding a little victory in something as simple as the starting of a car was the kind of attitude and gratefulness we would need to be successful in our endeavors... in our quest.

Soon we had coasted down the gravel drive and popped out onto the desolate and abandoned two lane highway. I kept the buggy in low gear to keep the cold wind at a minimum and to give me time to think as we rolled ever closer to the edge of the city. Without a word, Daniel pointed to a blue, square highway sign that only had an 'H' on it with an arrow. We took the exit and drove through a short distance of empty suburbs that ended abruptly. Commercial businesses and buildings grew larger and more frequent. We had found our way into downtown Bakersfield and, following the informational signs, I knew we were closing in on the hospital that Daniel knew of... probably all too well.

"Notice anything odd?" Elle leaned over and spoke in a flat and emotionless tone.

"Yeah... there's nobody here... like nobody." I had been thinking the same thing she had, I believe.

"Right, and no destruction either... like no Titan tracks." She took a horrific thing and twisted it just enough to make me smile inside. She was definitely my kinda twisted.

"Do you think everybody had some kind of warning and got out of town?" Daniel proposed something that Elle and I hadn't thought of, and it actually gave me a glimmer of hope.

"Well, let's keep looking around. Maybe we'll figure out where they went." I suggested, raising my voice slightly to talk over the echo of the rumbling exhaust from the dune buggy.

"THERE!" Daniel pointed over the rooftops of the buildings.

I expected to see a Titan looming ominously over the cityscape, but Daniel was excitedly pointing out the overlapping 'C C C ' sign on the side of towering building, only a few blocks away. It was the easily recognized logo of the California Cancer Center. I wasn't sure what good it would be to find a deserted hospital, and in my opinion, I thought we would be better off to find an abandoned grocery store, or an army surplus store... or a sporting goods store filled with guns and ammo. The thought made me chuckle to myself. Elle had carried a rifle on her back since we had met, and after busting it so badly in her horrible bike wreck that we couldn't be sure of being able to use it safely, we were now packing 9mm handguns, but not once had we fired a single shot.

"Well, I guess we're here," I said, pulling up to the main entrance to the hospital. I parked the Dune buggy in the middle of the street, knowing I wouldn't have to worry about traffic, or getting a ticket. I climbed out of the open rail buggy and was headed around to help Daniel and Elle climb out. Out of natural habit, I scanned across the front of the building when something caught my eye from above. I couldn't move, or talk. I stood there in the middle of the road like an idiot and stared upward. Of course, Daniel and Elle managed to get out of the passenger side just fine without me.

"Something wrong?" Elle asked with genuine concern.

"Whatcha lookin'..." Daniel began but stopped mid-sentence when he followed my gaze. He jumped into the air and waved his arms over his head joyously. "Hey!!! Down here!"

Elle looked up and was dumbfounded as well when she saw dozens of faces staring out of the hospital's fifth-floor windows.

"You know, they could all be Takers, right?" She had always been the sensible and cautious one, keeping me from danger more times than I cared to count.

"Good point." I dared not argue with this little spitfire. "That's why you'll wait here and Daniel and I will go check 'em out first."

"Right!" Daniel's ego grew a foot as my words transformed him from an introverted half-pint to a soldier of fortune, destined to protect the beautiful woman (who was usually the most intimidating one of us).

"Oh hell no!" Elle's voice twanged in sarcastic anger. "Let me make one thing perfectly clear... if you think I'm just gonna sit here and wait like a helpless 'girlie-girl' till you bubble wrap everything, you must be out of your freakin' mind!" With the forceful statement and the sound of ripping Velcro, she whipped out her 9mm and even with her arm in a sling, one thing was certain. She. Was. Bad. Ass.

"That's cool with me, but I'm still going in first." I knew I couldn't stop her, even if I wanted to.

"Whatevs!" She laughed and pushed past me. "If they aren't Takers, and they're armed, you'll just get shot... again."

"Ouch," Daniel said quietly and earned a wink from Elle.

"Okay, okay... let's just go." I threw my hands in the air and surrendered to her demands.

The three of us stood at the glass entrance, cupped our hands around our eyes and peered inside. Elle pushed and tugged at the powerless automatic door, but it would not open. I decided to try to help her since I had enhanced strength, but no matter how we tried, it was to no avail. These doors were not going to open.

"Guys!" Daniel squeaked.

Several figures had assembled in the shadows of the main corridor. Their movement was slow as they swayed side to side ever so slightly. My first thought was that we had a building full of trapped Takers with no Ahsusha to lead them. The first to step forward from the shadow into the daylight filled lobby of the center was a short and sturdy looking middle-aged woman, dressed in blue pants and duck print scrubs. She moved toward us hesitantly and it seemed clear to me, she did not have the 'crack-head' look or the empty gray eyes of the Takers.

"Ms. Shelly! It's me!" Daniel bellowed out, waving frantically to the woman inside.

The woman raised her hands to her mouth in shock and then rushed up to the glass.

"Go around..." She said a complete and lengthy sentence, but her words were silent to us. I could lip read the first two words and she motioned and pointed to her left, repeatedly. With somewhat of an understanding of what she wanted, I herded my companions in the

126

direction 'Ms. Shelly' had directed. I looked for some reason for us to be heading in this direction, some sign, but I didn't see anything.

"Where are we going, Big D?" I thought maybe he could shed some light on where we were supposed to be going.

"Heck if I know." Daniel shrugged his shoulder and his eyes widened.

"Over here!" A woman's voice came from around the corner of the main entrance.

We followed her words and found Ms. Shelly leaning out of a tan painted, steel, service door. She motioned us inside, and her eyes grew wide when she saw Elle's handgun drawn and the faint green glow in my pupils, surrounded by the dead-giveaway gray that surrounded them.

"Daniel? Is that you?" Her eyes teared up. "Oh... my little buddy... What happened to you?" She was beyond distraught when she saw that the boy had the same strange eyes as I had. "Can you understand me?"

"Duh, Ms. Shelly. I'm a little different, but I didn't go stupid." He said, sounding more like a thirteen-year-old than he had since we had met. "I think I got better... oh, these are my new friends, Ms. Elle, and Mr. Tanner." Ms. Shelly half nodded to us, making eye contact for a fraction of a second.

"Dear lord!" She gently rustled her fingers through his wispy blonde hair. "Let's go up and see Dr. Green. He'll be so happy to see you." She smiled and though her awkward uncomfortableness was obvious, she placed her arm around his shoulder. "You know what?"

"I guess not..." The fuzzy headed boy was unsure how to respond to her question. After all, he knew quite a bit more than he did before... in fact, there were some things he knew that he was sure Ms. Shelly did not know.

"A lot of your friends are here. Alyssa and Kyle are up here, and Brandon and Victoria..." She was growing slightly more comfortable with Daniel's unusual changes, but she continually looked over her shoulder to keep an eye on Elle and me. She even *held the door* for Elle and me when we reached the stairwell, allowing us to go first, where she could constantly watch us.

The stairwell was built of the typical cinder-block walls that were painted a putrid, pale, 1963 green and had a narrow rectangular window on each landing that let just enough daylight into despise the tasteless color-scheme. The metal stringers, risers, and handrails were dingy, off white color; almost eggshell, not quite beige, but a dirty looking color, as if it hadn't always been so. Darkened paths, where grimy shoe soles had traveled, stained the concrete of the steps and landings. Our footsteps echoed hauntingly in the otherwise silent tower as we climbed higher and higher. Each landing had a single steel door, painted the same dull off-white color as the metal handrails. Dirty marks and smudges from the natural oils of countless hands discolored the areas along the edge of the door and around the doorknob and each door was adorned with a hand painted number to announce the floor.

"Stop up here at the fifth floor." Ms. Shelly announced as we passed the metal door marked with a faded, '4' on it, denoting the entrance to the fourth floor.

"Ms. Shelly, maybe you and 'Big D' should go first." Elle was right. If a strange man with alien eyes and a handgun-toting woman entered first, we might not be met with a friendly welcome.

"You can just call me Shelly." The nurse looked down, almost embarrassed, and smiled. "That's probably a good idea."

Elle and I stopped on the fifth-floor landing and let the nurse and former patient go first. Nurse Shelly pulled the door open and held it for Daniel. I took the door after she entered and held it open for Elle and me to enter behind them. The corridor was much nicer than the stairway and had been updated recently with fresh paint and carpet and beautifully finished wooden doors and trim. Most of the doors were propped open to allow light from the windows in each room to drift out into the hallway. At the far end of this wing of the fifth floor, I could see an open common area, like a waiting room. The front wall was a glass curtain-wall, where I had figured we had spotted the watchers when we stood in the street out front, but now, not a single person was in sight.

"Doctor Green?" Nurse Shelly called out loudly and her voice echoed down the empty hospital wing. "We have visitors." She seemed as if she were searching and hoping, unsure if she would get an answer. "Doctor Green!" She shouted. "You won't believe who's here to see you, doc!"

"Who is it Shelly?" A male voice came from somewhere in the distance, but before Shelly could answer, a short, stubby, male nurse rounded the corner and then stopped abruptly when he saw the four of us, though most likely his biggest shock was the sight of my and Daniel's eyes, glowing in the dimly lit corridor. He was dressed from head to toe in burgundy colored scrubs. His chubby, round face sported a van-dyke style beard. He wore thick black plastic framed glasses, and what little hair he had was short, black and surrounded a large bald patch, with one thin tuft that stuck out high on his forehead. His mouth hung open wide for a moment before he attempted to speak again. "Is that...?"

"Yep, it's me, Daniel!" The boy answered before he could finish his question. Daniel rushed up to the man and wrapped him in a heartfelt hug. "I missed you, Mr. Bill." But what Daniel really meant was that it was good to find someone, who had cared for him and been a friend to him when he was at his sickest, alive and seemingly untouched by the alien apocalypse.

"Danny boy!" Bill cried out. "Since when did you have more hair than me?"

"Since I turned into an alien...AAARRGGG!" Daniel stuck his bottom jaw out, put his arms out in front of him and stepped back and forth like Frankenstein's monster. Nurse Bill grabbed the boy up in his arms and hugged him again and growled a goofy growl, which caused Daniel to giggle uncontrollably.

"I thought I heard laughter out here. Did somebody..." The tall, thin, silver-haired man appeared in the hallway, dressed in tan slacks and a button down shirt. "Oh my god..."

"Dr. Green..." Shelly began. "You remember Daniel Martin? The last time you saw him was about a month ago. He came by for a visit and to show off his new hair. And... he brought a couple of his friends with him. This is Tanner and Elle, sorry I didn't get your last names." She rambled on so quickly we couldn't even respond. "This is Dr. Alan Green, and that's Bill, or Billy, Smitts."

"Pleased to meet you all," I said and Elle nodded silently, holstering her handgun. Dr. Green stared in shock as if I had snakes coming out of my ears.

"Hi, Doc!" Daniel said exuberantly.

"Well, hello son. How are you feeling today?" Even though the world had been invaded by ginormous alien crafts and the entire city had apparently been stripped of its citizens by zombie, alien takers, Dr. Green could not deviate from his canned rhetoric.

"I'm feelin' pretty awesome, but..." The boy surprised Dr. Green by his effervescent attitude. "I am kinda hungry."

"I'm not sure what exactly has transpired, but I believe something unprecedented has happened." He spoke in a monotone voice that was neither alarming or calming. "Let's go down to the cafeteria and get you all something to eat and drink. Would you be willing to tell me about what has brought you here and in the state that you are currently in?"

"Of course," I said and smiled at him to show I was an ally. "There's a lot to tell," Daniel grinned when I spoke, knowing that he and I had a library of alien information stored somewhere deep in our brains.

"Did someone mention food? Because I'm, like, starving." Elle rubbed her stomach and for the first time I really noticed she had the clichéd *baby bump,* but it was even a bit more than just a bump.

"That reminds me." I knew it was a cancer hospital, but I knew this might be the only medical professionals we would find. "Elle might be... well, she's probably..."

"Oh, I'm definitely." She chuckled and cocking her head to the side directed her statement to Dr. Green. "I'm pregnant... with... *his* baby."

"Well..." The doctor was once again in shock and unsure how to respond.

"Come on this way." Nurse Shelly interjected. "Back down to the second floor and we'll rustle you up something to eat."

Our morale was up as we descended the stairs and found our way to the cafeteria. The large open space was set up as three restaurants that surrounded a comfortable and aesthetically pleasing dining area. Of course, the restaurants were not functional and I wondered what Nurse Shelly might offer us for an early lunch. As with the waiting area on the fifth floor, the wall opposite of the serving and ordering lines was comprised entirely of glass and overlooked the barren city.

"Sit wherever you want and I'll be right back," Shelly smiled politely, still somewhat uncomfortable with the *new people*.

"Do you need a hand?" Elle offered and Shelly graciously accepted the help from the one new person whose eyes did not look eerily alien.

The dining area was designed to be relaxing and comforting. The ceiling, bulkheads, and even the floor pattern, that was partially commercial grade carpet and partly parquet, wood flooring, were comprised of soft, curved lines. The tables ranged from small square tables for two and large oval tables that could seat as many as ten. They were different shapes and sizes, but all were made of the same materials and in that way matched. I chose a smaller oval table near the glass curtain wall of windows. I took a seat in one of the chairs, which were very modern, armless and all of them were identical... and though they looked quite comfortable, they were not. Daniel and Dr. Green joined me and our conversation began.

"So, doc... I guess this is all pretty weird, huh?" I broke the silence and waved my hand in a circle around my face, initiating the *talk* that I knew Dr. Green was dying to have.

"I suppose *weird* is one way to describe it though I was thinking more that it was fascinating." The doctor rubbed the stubbly beard that was forming on his careworn face. "I am guessing by the look of your eyes," he referenced Daniel and I both. "...that you were supposed to be used like one of the people the aliens took over, but you have somehow managed to keep your humanity. Is that an accurate assumption?"

"Sort of, I guess," Daniel answered him before I could speak.

"Do you think that the alien beings inside of you could completely take you over at some point, in the way that they have the others?" Dr., Green raised a valid concern that I hadn't even considered.

"Honestly, I hadn't thought of that, but what happened to us is a little different than what happened to everyone else." I wasn't sure how to explain it other than rehashing the entire story of my encounter with the Ahsusha. Daniel told his story when I had finished, and even though Dr. Green wanted to stop us and ask a dozen questions, he waited until

133

we had finished before bombarding us with his thoughts, ideas, and question.

"So Daniel, let me get this straight." Dr. Green began. "You started feeling better and your hair started to regrow right after your *encounter* with the alien?"

"Yep. As soon as it died, or whatever, I felt a lot better. Like within a couple of minutes I felt like I could run." Daniel smiled at his doctor. "I haven't felt that good in over a year."

"I want to run a blood test, if you will allow it, Daniel." Dr. Green stated as if it were a simple thing.

"Can you do that without power?" I asked curiously, knowing nothing about the medical field.

"No, I can't, but our maintenance department has a few gas powered generators that we use from time to time, only when we have to." He had a foxy grin as he spoke.

"You aren't telling us everything, are you?" I pried.

"As I am sure you aren't telling me everything either." He shot a sideways glance at me, and his statement made Daniel chuckle.

"There is a lot to tell, doc. How much time do you have?" I answered and winked at Daniel.

"It feels like time is all we really have right now." He had a point. "As far as what I *wasn't telling you*... I think there may be a correlation between the malignant tumor in Daniel's brain and the alien's inability to survive when it tried to take him over. Have you ever been diagnosed with any form of cancer, Tanner?"

"Not that I know of, but I don't have many memories from before the invasion." I was being mostly honest, but I had an immediate flashback to the airplane dream and the words my *wife* had used to comfort me. It was possible that the answers and help she talked about were in reference to some type of cancer.

"Lunch is served!" Elle called out as she and Shelly pushed out of a set of double swinging doors.

"Bring it on!" Daniel yelled out cheerily.

The women brought out two large, red plastic serving trays. Setting the trays down on the table beside us, they began passing out nicely prepared salads, a variety of dressing packets and offered a variety of soft drinks and snack-size chip bags. Elle and Shelly had also prepared turkey sandwiches with lettuce and onion on thickly sliced whole wheat bread. It was not the Genesis feast we had enjoyed earlier that week, but it looked delicious. The two ladies joined us at the table and Dr. Green gave Ms. Shelly a brief overview of our conversation.

"Well, that is an amazing story," Shelly remarked. "I can't imagine what it's like out there. We've kept ourselves locked in here since the aliens showed up and just took everyone else. That was what?... weeks ago now?" The doctor nodded and I could tell he was remembering the world before and probably family and friends that were so senselessly ripped from the world.

"Until you showed up today, we thought we might be the only people left." The doctor spoke solemnly. "Are there others?"

"Yeah..." Elle interjected. "Didn't you tell him about Barnhill?"

"I hadn't told him everything yet." I wasn't holding any information from him intentionally. "You and Nurse Shelly weren't gone that long."

"So..." Elle gave me a look that meant something, but as was usual, I wasn't that good at nonverbal cues. "I'm guessing he doesn't know about Maddie either, then..."

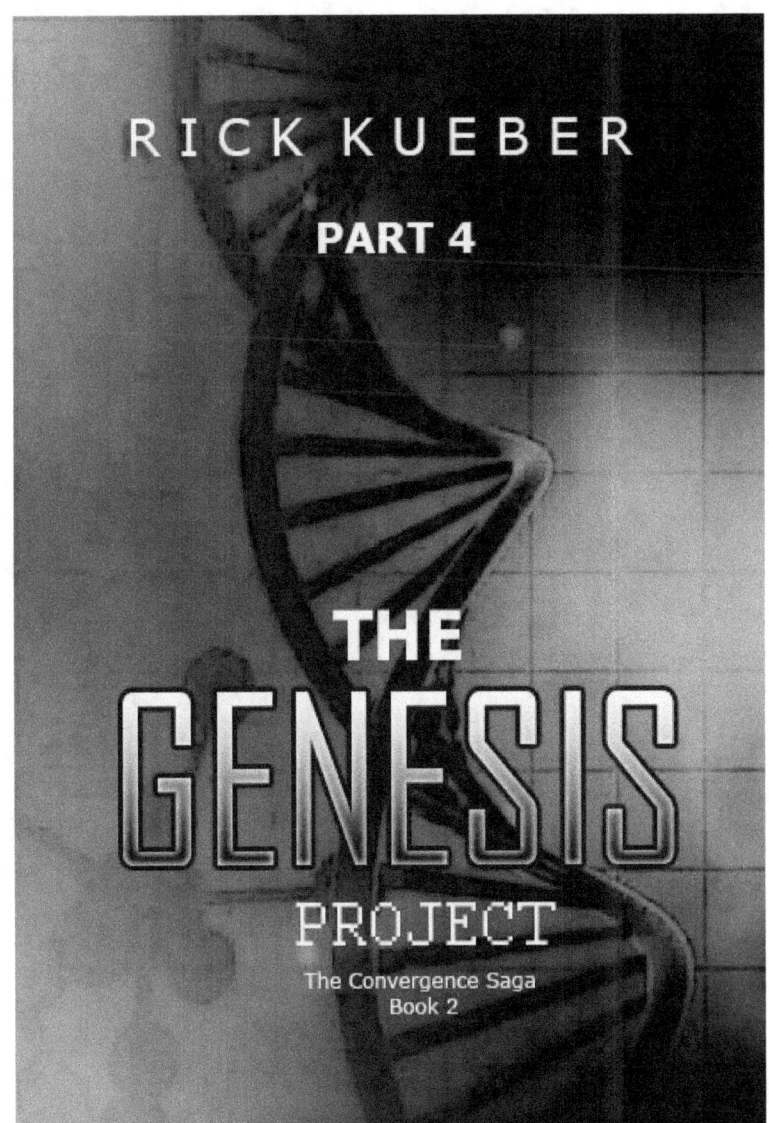

Chapter 10

Discovery

"Who is this Maddie?" Dr. Green's curiosity was immediately peaked by Elle's question.

Elle told the story of how she had found Maddie and her mother Tory, the abridged version of our travels from the cave to the cabins and eventually how we came to find Barnhill. The story of how Maddie and I were both shot by an honest case of mistaken identity was told in much greater detail.

"I can completely understand that." Shelly tossed in amidst the storytelling. "If I had a gun, and I didn't recognize Daniel, I might have shot you too!"

"And I guess I couldn't have blamed you," Elle answered before continuing her story. "Tanner healed unnaturally swiftly... overnight. The Titan came back with the Takers, the alien people, and Tanner was separated from us for a few weeks. When he returned, Maddie was not doing well. We believed that she had an infection that spread to her bloodstream and was about to die."

Dr. Green was completely enthralled and Nurse Shelly gasped. "That poor child."

"Yes, we didn't know what to do. We kept her medicated a little with painkillers and antibiotics, but it only slowed the infection a little. By the time Tanner returned, she was only hours away from death and we decided to try the unthinkable. Tanner had been hurt and healed quickly more than once due to his being part alien, and so some of his blood was drawn and injected straight into her." Elle told the story well, but I could tell that it was making her miss Maddie, and we had only been gone for a little more than a day.

"But that could have killed her if it was the wrong blood type." Shelly exasperated.

"We didn't have much choice. She was dying already." I explained our reasoning again.

"So, what happened to the girl?" Dr. Green was an oncology

specialist, an academic genius, but Elle had him on the edge of his uncomfortable seat.

"She began to get better," Elle smiled. "She started getting better quickly, and she had a new glimmer in her eyes."

"A glimmer?" The doc asked. "Like hope?"

"She had hope, and she gave us all hope, but no... what I meant was that when she awoke, her beautiful eyes looked like they were filled with a glitter that twinkled with a pale green color," Elle explained.

"I'd like to do a blood test on you too, Mr. Tanner if you'd be willing." Dr. Green proposed, but I knew he had something cooking in his 'Magna Cum Laude' brain.

"It's actually *Mr. Astin*." I corrected him before I realized that this may have been meant in the same way the Mr. Bill and Ms. Shelly were so named. "My full name is Tanner Astin and this is..." That was the moment I realized I was sitting with a woman who was carrying my unborn child, and I never even knew her last name. My face went pale.

"Elle." She stated stiffly.

"Just Elle?" Nurse Shelly raised an eyebrow. "My name is Shelly Rush. Surely you have a last name."

"You never told us your last name either." Elle directed her statement to Daniel and intentionally tried to divert the focus from herself.

"Then you weren't listening that well upstairs...Daniel Andrew Martin." Shelly shot back quickly. "So, about your name..."

"Okay, fine... if you must know, my name is Elu Yatokya." Elle looked irritated. "So that's why I go by just *Elle*."

"That's beautiful." Shelly tried to be encouraging but didn't know what else to say.

"Native American, right?" Dr. Green asked and took Elle by surprise. "Choctaw?"

"Actually, it's Zuni. Most people have never heard of our tribe. If you aren't Cherokee, some people don't know you're Native American."

"It is beautiful," I smiled at the woman I had fallen in love with. It seemed like a lifetime ago when she found me in the desert. "Does it translate to Elle?" Everyone seemed shocked that I was asking questions to the mother of my future child.

"No, I just like Elle. It actually means Earth and Sun in Zuni." She seemed suddenly proud of her native heritage, and it came to me that she had always had some sort of unique ethnicity about her, but I never questioned it. She had saved my life more than once, she was beautiful and caring, and I loved her. Where her ancestors were from was immaterial.

We chatted about more everyday things while we finished our lunch and then proceeded down the stairs to the second floor where all of the hospital labs were located. Instead of taking us into the typical exam room, the doc whispered into Shelly's ear and then showed us into a breakroom. Elle, Daniel and I sat down at the break table and watched as Dr. Green began to rummage through the cabinets. "Aha!" he exclaimed after opening the cabinet under the sink and retrieving a container of disinfecting bleach wipes. He pulled almost a half dozen wipes from the canister and began to scrub the entire table three times.

"I think I got everything here." Shelly shouted out as she pushed her way through the door.

"Whatcha got there?" I asked as she placed a stainless steel tray covered in a blue, heavy cotton cloth on the table in front of us.

"I hope it's everything I need to take a few blood samples and some blood test kits." Dr. Green answered, peeking under the cloth. "While we already have Daniel's blood type on file, I'd like to retest it to see if there are any changes that our basic test kits could pick up on. I also would like to take a few samples from each of you to examine. I can verify that you are in fact pregnant and perhaps I can learn a little more about the changes that have occurred to you, Tanner and Daniel."

"That would be great, but I haven't had any changes, just those two," Elle responded to the doctor.

"You may be right, but it wouldn't hurt to have a look." He was extremely calm though we could see a fire in his eyes. "We might be on the verge of a medical breakthrough here... a miracle in fact."

"I suppose you're right." Elle was afraid that Dr. Green might find something. She was dealing well with my being some sort of a hybrid and was doing her best not to worry about the child she believed she carried, but to think that carrying this child may be affecting her own biology was something she was not prepared to face.

"Well, no time like the present." Dr. Green smiled.

"Okay, who would like to be first?" Nurse Shelly asked politely but made eye contact with me.

"I'd be happy to unless anyone else wants to go first." I volunteered.

I looked to my pair of traveling companions, but neither of them spoke up, so I laid my arm across the table and watched as the doc scrubbed it down with a disinfecting wipe. He snapped on a pair of latex gloves, uncovered the tray and fingered through the instruments while my arm dried. Picking up a collection tube and needle, he tore open the sterile packaging and assembled the two pieces. Nurse Shelly wrapped a rubber tourniquet around my upper arm and tied it snugly. She tapped my arm following the typical procedure, even though my veins were more than visible. The tiniest beads of sweat appeared on Dr. Green's forehead as he tore open a package containing an alcohol swab and began to scrub over my protruding vein in a circular motion.

"You're going to feel a little pinch." Dr. Green spoke one of the most frequently told lies in the medical profession. He pulled the skin taught over my pulsing vein and with a swift poke, stuck the needle in my arm. "First, try!" He exclaimed. "Not bad for someone who isn't a phlebotomist."

"And I didn't feel a thing." I countered the doctor's lie with one of my own.

I watched as the stubby test tube shaped vial filled with my dark red, liquid of life. Nurse Shelly took over and swapped out the vials, filling a second one before removing the tourniquet and slipping the needle from my arm. She placed a square of gauze over the puncture point and taped it in place with the clinical, white paper tape that rarely held longer than a few minutes. While she took care of my arm, the doc removed the needle from the vial, slipped it into a 'sharps' container, placed a cap on tightly and placed a sticker label on it that had *Tanner* handwritten across it, just like the first vial.

"Who's next?" Shelly smiled and looked over to Daniel.

"I guess I am." Daniel knew he was being called out and responded with an extreme lack of enthusiasm. The procedure was repeated and then repeated again. When the three of us had been stuck, slightly bruised and bandaged, Dr. Green handed the tray containing the unused test kits and the labeled vials to Shelly.

"Would you take this to the blood lab and just leave it at the first station? I'll head there in a minute." He nodded to the nurse politely.

"Of course doctor." She answered professionally. "And I'll see you three in a minute and we'll head back upstairs. Hospital beds aren't the most comfortable, but we can find you a room that should suffice." and with that she disappeared out into the hallway.

"So, my new friends..." Dr. Green began. "What do you think of this 'there really is intelligent alien life' surprise?"

"My odd amnesia may be affecting how I see it, but it seems like something I always expected. Maybe not in the way that it happened, but I think I always thought we weren't alone." The words tumbled out of my mouth without thinking.

"I think it'd be cool if everyone wasn't dead," Daniel said sorely.

"You are an amazing young man." Elle took his hand and tried to comfort him. "Not everyone would have survived the way you did."

"Maybe I just survived because I was dying, and everybody that wasn't dying, did..." Daniel had an angry, but not hateful tone.

"Well, Daniel... maybe your surviving can help others. That's what we're going to try to find out." The kind doctor tried to give Daniel's upside down life purpose. "So, now that we know, without a doubt, that we are not alone... did you ever think that maybe these visitors we have aren't the only other intelligent life out there?"

"I hadn't, I guess," Elle answered in such a quiet whisper, it seemed she was mumbling to herself and was deep in thought. "You don't think there are other aliens on their way here, do you?"

"Not likely." Dr. Green eased our minds with his simple opinion, even though a year ago, his opinion would have been that we would never be visited by alien life, and that sure as hell would have been wrong. "But, it does make one think."

"Yes it does." I searched my mind for a reason to believe other alien beings might soon be invading the earth, but I had no hidden information regarding that.

"Well, I had better get started testing those blood samples." He stood up, shook my hand and nodded to Daniel and Elle. "I will see you all upstairs later this evening." And with that, he left the three of us alone.

"So, do we wait here, or go upstairs?" I asked Elle's opinion.

"I guess we could do whatever we want. No one said we had to wait here." She pondered the options and patted her holster. "Besides, we have the guns. I don't think anyone's going to stop us." Her words pulled a grin back to Daniel's scowling face.

"Hey, you know what?" I asked Elle but wasn't able to answer my own question.

"Hello again!" Nurse Shelly burst into the room like a whirlwind. "Let's go upstairs so you can meet everyone else. There's some comfy couches and chairs up there too... much better than these hard old things." She referenced the hard, unpadded, stack-able, breakroom chairs.

"Sounds good to me." Elle groaned as she stood up, nursing her still sore arm.

"What happened to you, girl?" The nurse asked with concern. "We could have had Dr. Green look at that, but I can take a look at it when we get upstairs."

Elle and the nurse talked amongst themselves about the bike accident and how and where her shoulder hurt while we climbed the countless stairs to the fifth floor. Daniel and I stayed a few steps behind them to avoid running into them, as they stopped frequently when something in their conversation begged for their undivided attention. Being the *men* in the group, we found ourselves silently smiling to each other and rolling our eyes with every 'Oh, girl' and 'Let me tell you' that was said. When we reached the fifth floor, I pushed past everyone and held the door for them. This time, the wing of the cancer center was not so silent or dismal. Though we did not see anyone right away, this floor of the hospital was now buzzing with the sounds of muffled conversations and carts wheeling down laminate flooring nearby. We were led by Shelly to the waiting area at the end of the corridor. Dozens of patients and several of the staff dressed in a variety of colored scrubs mobbed us when they realized we had returned.

Elle and I sat on one of the couches and soon we were surrounded by inquisitive minds of every age and background. Daniel had found a group of young people who he had become friends with when he had begun his treatments. Questions of 'What's it like out there?', 'How did you survive?', 'Are you an alien?' and 'Have you seen those things up close?" fluttered from the mouths of patients and staff alike. It was uncomfortable at first, but soon we realized, to them we looked like the heroes from one of those zombie apocalypse shows. We chatted all afternoon and into the evening until the new wore off and our *groupies* began to trickle away. Elle and I told some of our stories, but others were saved for us alone to know. Though we didn't speak of them, I could feel that we both knew exactly which tales to tell and which to withhold.

When the sun set, it seemed to be the routine for nearly everyone to turn in. Even without power, the nurses and orderlies maintained a strict schedule for therapies and medicines. The patients, and some of their family members who were fortunate enough to have been in the hospital when the Titans used their EMP weapon to disable all sources of power and the Takers flooded the city were kept separated by floor and wing according to their particular type of cancer. Rooms had been designated on each floor for the staff to take turns sleeping. When the night shift took over, we were faced with a repeat of questions and queries, but we didn't mind. This group of unlikely survivors looked to us with hope and if we were able to give even a glimmer of hope in these dark times, that was an unequaled reward.

***

"I don't know about you, but I'm about ready for some sleep," I said to Elle, Daniel and the small assemblage that still surrounded us in the darkened waiting room.

"Me too." She leaned into me like butter melting into hot toast and nuzzled her face against my shoulder and chest.

"Not me..." Daniel argued. "I'm not tired at all!"

"Tired or not, you better get to resting up. We get up with the sun around here." A very petite night shift nurses coaxed.

"Are there any empty beds, or should we sleep out here?" I started to ask, but the sound of an opening door and the flickering of light from down the corridor distracted us from the path of our current conversation. We stared at the light that danced off of the pattern less, vinyl wall covering awaiting the revelation of what its source might be.

"Oh good! You're still awake!" Dr. Green bantered as he rounded the corner carrying an LED light strip and entered the waiting area. "I have some interesting discoveries to share with you."

"Oh, hey doc! Where the hell did you get that light?" Elle beat me to the punch.

"This?" He held up the light. It was about a foot long, held dozens of high output LED bulbs, and it was housed in a yellow plastic case with a hooked hangar on one end. "My wife gave this to me on my last birthday.

I didn't want it to sit in the garage gathering dust and hurt her feelings, so I brought it to work where it could gather dust... out of sight, out of mind, you know?"

"That's a sweet story, but how?" Elle prodded a bit deeper. "I mean, I haven't seen a single working battery since..."

"Oh, right!" He turned it around, but with the bulbs facing the other way, Elle could see nothing. I, on the other hand, had an incredible epiphany just as he explained his action. "It's got this handy solar strip on the back side, so I hang it from one of the window blinds all day and presto, a good three hours of light each night, but I try not to use it. We don't want to attract any unwanted attention."

"I was just about to show them to a couple of empty patient rooms where they could sleep for the night." The male nurse explained to the doctor.

"It is getting a little late, I suppose." He rubbed his forehead. "How about you take Daniel to his room and then come back for these two?"

"Do I have to?" Daniel whined.

"It's probably best. We have a lot of work to do tomorrow, but I will let you in on one of my discoveries." The doctor's smile was very comforting as he wrapped his arm around Daniel's shoulder. "I looked over a sample of your blood with a fine toothed comb and I don't see any of the queues that would suggest cancer was present. You may very well be a living miracle."

"I guess I can go to bed if I have to," Daniel smiled and was suddenly less reluctant. He even gave his former doctor a gentle, one armed, shoulder squeezing hug before wandering off into the darkness with his escort.

"I'd like a word with you two." He directed his words to Elle and me but looked around at the others that were mustered around the cold glow of the LEDs. "...alone."

Chapter 11
A New Beginning

We followed the doctor to the nurse's station, away from the others, where we could talk more privately. Apprehension weighed on me as I awaited and expected dark and dangerous words to spew from the shadowy doctor's lips. Elle, on the other hand, seemed very cool and unwavering by the doctor's, yet unknown, disclosures. The doctor placed his light face down on the table, placing a dim under-glow on the surrounding desk and chairs.

"Have a seat." He gestured kindly to the three seats that sat before us.

"Okay." I pulled out the center, rolling office chair and offered it to Elle. She said 'thank you' with only the smile in her eyes.

"What's this all about, then?" Elle's whispery voice was as sultry as I had heard it, and as much as I wanted to know what the doc had to say, I wanted nothing more than to kiss her right at that very moment.

"I have run several tests on the blood samples, as you heard me telling young Daniel, I'm sure." He and I sat down on either side of Elle and the three of us huddled together like school children telling ghost stories around a flashlight. Unfortunately, I have limited resources here. Many of our test samples are sent off for more detailed analysis. That is a luxury that we no longer have."

"Come on doc... get to the point." I had already scooted to the edge of my seat and the anticipation and anxiety were killing me. "We can 'talk shop' later. Tell us what you know first, then you can tell us what you don't."

"What I know without any doubts is that Elle is type 'O', Daniel is, as I had already known, type 'AB negative'. You on the other hand..."

"Me what?" I nearly fell forward, out of my chair.

"Your blood looks like any other under a microscope, but it does not react with any of the markers on the test kits." He frowned. "I am... puzzled. And not to sound arrogant, but that is saying something."

"So, it's like the rest of him..." Elle rubbed her hand across my thigh to comfort me. "... he looks normal, but he is extraordinary and an enigma."

"Yes, I suppose that is one way to put it." The doctor had a good 'bedside manner' but was still a bit dry. "Also, Elle, you are indeed and without a doubt, pregnant, but I would venture to guess that your enlarged abdomen alerted you to that reality already. I hope you plan to stay a while so that we can monitor your progress."

"We hadn't really thought about it, but we could maybe stay for a little while." Elle liked the thought of being under the watchful eye of medical professionals, considering she knew very little about being pregnant.

"Maybe for a little while, but we can't stay long." I felt an urgency to our quest, no matter how unsure it was. Elle shot me a look of displeasure and I quickly changed the subject. "Is there anything else?"

"Well I suppose there is something, but I am not positive about it yet." He seemed distant. "Without modern technology I am afraid to act on it, but I can't help but wonder what might happen if we gave those here that are battling cancer an injection like you had done with the young girl."

"I'd be more than willing to try, but I can't say if that was a one in a million shot, or not." I could afford to donate a little blood if it meant that I might be able to help others.

"I find it very odd that your blood is indiscriminate, but Daniel's is unchanged from when he was here. You both had the same experience that caused your.... changes?" He fumbled to not offend.

"Yes, we did." I began to relax, sitting back in my chair a little. "As far as I can tell."

"Tomorrow." Dr. Green stood up. "We'll talk more tomorrow after I make my morning rounds."

"You finished with these two, Dr. Green?" The diminutive nurse had reappeared without warning.

"Yes. We're all wrapped up for the night." Dr. Green stood up and picked up his light, taking it with him down the hall. "I'll catch up with you in the morning."

153

From the sixth floor, an empty patient room with two beds was calling to us. While we had been busy, Mr. Bill had bravely ventured out to our buggy and unloaded our luggage, packing it all of the way up to the fifth-floor waiting room. Elle and I shouldered our packs, snatched up the suitcases and deeply anticipated a good night's sleep. Directed by the half-pint nurse, I led the way. The surroundings were more visible to me in the tiniest of starlight that drifted in through the windows, but it did not seem that they were quite as bright or clear as they had been. My mind wandered through the possibilities briefly, but I quickly shut down my doubts, telling myself it was simply the fact that there was virtually no light at all to perceive. After a short climb of steps, we entered a corridor that we had not been in before, even though it was a mirror image of the floor below. The tiny nurse pushed ahead and immediately placed herself halfway through a doorway just to our right.

"Here you go. There are two beds in here unless you'd prefer separate rooms." Her hand was outstretched as if to offer the room to us.

"One room is fine... perfect in fact." Elle's hand slipped across my chest and she felt her way to the wall and then to the door frame. "We've slept on a rock, under a rock, and inside of a rock. This might as well be the Ritz, as far as I'm concerned."

"Thank you," I whispered as I entered, close behind Elle.

The curtain was drawn to divide the two beds and the room smelled of disinfectant and laundered linen. Extra blankets, the scratchy kind no one likes unless they are freezing, and flat, stiff pillows were neatly stacked in the two institutional looking chairs that were pushed up against the wall at the foot of the beds. I offered Elle her choice, and she decided on the bed nearest the door, leaving me with the window view.

It was chilly in the room, but I still stripped completely down and slipped on a pair of silky black basketball shorts. Reaching for an extra blanket, I caught a glimpse of Elle behind the curtain. She had removed every stitch of clothing, having worn it all for the past two days. Her silhouette was magnificent, baby bump and all. With her arms over her head to slip into an oversized t-shirt from her backpack, her supple breasts were outlined against the pasty white walls. The hollow of the small of her back curved perfectly into her well-rounded bottom, and just as the t-shirt fell to hide the paradise below it, I noticed that when she stretched her body in just the right way, two tiny dimples materialized at the top of her hips.

"Goodnight beautiful." I stole behind her and whispered in her ear, placing my hands on her hips and letting them wander until they met at the underside of her belly, feeling the inner curves of her hipbones against my wrists.

"Sleep well." Her words were so panted and breathy they were barely audible. The tense muscles in my neck and shoulders relaxed and my head eased downward until my lips came to rest where Elle's neck and shoulder met. My lips opened and then puckered, making a quiet smacking noise as I softly kissed her tawny skin. Reluctantly I withdrew myself from the warmth and magnetism of her sensuality and retreated to my cold and hard hospital bed mattress. From beyond the veil of the divider curtain, I heard Elle suspire deeply, almost in a regretful moan. I heard the rustling of itchy blankets, stiff linens, and vinyl wrapped mattresses as Elle settled in.

I rolled away from the curtain and faced the window, staring out to the brilliant star lights that were pinpointed in the night sky. Silently I laid there listening to the sound of my whole world breathing heavily as she passed into her dream world. The rhythmic sound was like music, soothing me into my own blissful slumber.

***

Memory or dream, I cannot say which it was, but my heart wanted to believe it was a memory, came back to visit as I floated in the oblivion between conscious thought and dreamy sleep: *A humming-buzzing sound grew louder, waking me in the mid-night hours. A throbbing ache in my head had me dizzy-headed and sick to my stomach. Part of me just wanted to die to end the pain, and another part of me was praying to God, harder than I had ever prayed before, to ease my pain. There were blinding white lights inside of my head. No matter how hard I squeezed my eyes closed, the lights grew brighter and more intense until I could stand it no longer.*

Tormented beyond my limits, I jumped from my bed and stood facing my windows. I threw my eyes and mouth open wide, but the screams of agony that welled up from my soul would not come out. The pain in my head vanished and my world went black, both in my sightless eyes and in my mind. Standing frozen in terror, I wondered if I had just died and this was the truth of death's experience. Moments passed like hours, when finally a tiny dot of light, like a distant star appeared and just as it began to grow larger, it burst into three points of light, but each part seemed as large as the whole. I wanted to wake up from this nightmare of my own death. I wanted to crawl back into my bed and hide under my covers. I begged for the ultimate migraine to return to me and validate my life not being over. The three luminous globes of light drew close to me, and while I was partly relieved that their glow illuminated the room around me, mostly, I was frightened by these ghostly lights that had begun to swirl around me like iridescent pixies, sprinkling me with their magical stardust until my feet floated off of the floor.

I did not drift through an open window, or ethereally pass through a solid wall but like the changing of a radio station on an old style radio, my world became visually staticy and when it was unrecognizable like that point of radio static completely between radio stations, the three spheres of light exploded in a blinding flash and then the staticy vision returned and a completely new and queer station came in tune. Nothing was familiar. The sounds that hummed in the background or came in and out completely were like nothing my eardrums had ever processed... sounds so unique and alien that they seemed to have another dimension to them. There was an aroma that I had never experienced. It was not a pleasant smell, like that of a bakery in the morning, or appalling, like the scent of the corpses strewn across the small mountain town, but maybe it was more like something I might have accidentally discovered in my high school chemistry lab class. How do you explain experiencing things that transcend one's senses? The colors were few, but they were so vivid so surreal, it was as if each color had its own smell and taste that I could experience through sight alone, or perhaps this world had no single senses and all senses were somehow combined. I weighed the beauty of my experience with the curious thought that lacking a separation in senses could be very saddening in its own way. As I felt my body floating in this moment of 1960's trippy cognition, my senses all dulled at once into a dull grayish reality. The gray glow that overtook the very fabric of my being was depression personified. My heart and soul, my hopes and dreams sank with its presence. I could feel the gray infiltrating me... it soaked into my skin, penetrated my sight and hearing, I could taste its metallic sting in my mouth and feel it flooding my nostrils, like drowning, as I breathed it in. The spheres of luminescence reappeared just as I felt I was suffocating, about to die. The three became one and hovered directly in front of my face. I had no control over my body. I was literally paralyzed when the orbs of light became one and then opened up, exposing a dark secret, a horrible truth... a truth that I was on the verge of experiencing when I felt a tremor and the icy touch of an alien hand on the smooth, bare skin of my chest.

✱✱✱

"Wake up" A gentle voice whispered. "Are you okay?"

"Elle... is... is that you?" Panic took me and I could barely speak. "I can't see you."

"At least, you called me by the right name this time." She teased, but I could not find the humor in her sarcasm this time.

"No... really, I can't see you." I had taken my ability to see through the darkness for granted, and now it seemed to have been stolen from me while I slept in the night.

"I'm right here, baby." Her calloused hand caressed my cheek.

"I can hear you, but..." There was a sudden flutter of confusing lines, tangled and intertwined in an indiscernible, visible scribble. "Wait." I stopped myself and held my hand up, waving it back and forth in front of my face. There was a slight glow of fingered tracers. "I'm getting something."

"Can you see me at all?" Elle placed one hand on either side of my face. Her thumbs rested in the hollow below my cheekbones, her fingers slid into my tangled hair, that was growing longer by the week, and her pointer fingers rested on my temples. "Una hom." She spoke the two words like a poem or prayer, or some magical spell she was casting.

"There you are..." A calmness overtook me when Elle's eyes, only inches from mine, came into view. Then slowly her face, the tangles of her hair and then the rest of our surroundings. It all came to me in such a subtle way, like falling asleep... it happens, but so subtle and slowly that it is impossible to know the exact moment when it occurs. "What was that you said?"

"Oh, that?" My question seemed to make her slightly uncomfortable. "It was just something my mother used to say to me when she would wake me from a scary dream... 'Una hom"... it's Zuni for *see me*."

I placed my hand on the nape of her neck and pulled her in the last inch for a quick kiss. We lay down together in my bed, I, on my back and Elle on her side with her leg hung over me, her head on my chest and her injured arm placed gingerly across the tightened muscles of abdomen. The world outside was still dark and I wondered what time it was and how long I had slept, if I had slept... could it have been more than a dream?

"So, what happened?" I asked my lover nervously. "Why did you wake me?"

"You were shaking so hard it woke me up." She spoke into my chest. "I thought you were having a seizure or something. Your whole body was rigid and then you just went totally limp like a wet noodle. I was so scared and freaking out... I can't lose you. You made a promise, remember?"

"Yes, I remember." It was a memory that brought a serene feeling with it, and hope. "I will never leave you."

With those whispered words, Elle found comfort and soon found sleep once again, wrapped in my arm. I did not return to my slumber for fear of finding my nightmare again. Holding her close in my arms, I stared out of the window at the night sky, until the twilight began to lighten the city around us. Elle made moaning, mumbling noises and fidgeted in the confines of our tiny bed.

"Good morning princess." I stroked her hair softly and she stretched, long and tense, and then relaxed back against me.

"Morning..." She muttered almost unintelligibly. "Wonder if they have coffee here?"

Elle pushed against the bed, raising herself up and we began our day by getting dressed in our one spare outfit we had each packed. Jeans and a heavy, charcoal gray, fleece pullover warmed my body and the change of clothes refreshed my soul. Elle had changed into a white tank-top and a two-piece jogging suit, black with white stripes that ran down the outside of the legs and sleeves. As soon as we had dressed and stuffed our old clothes into a plastic laundry bag that Elle had found in the freestanding wardrobe, we ventured out of our room and down the stairs to the fifth floor to join the bustling group of survivors we had met the day before.

No sooner had we sat down in the waiting room than Nurse Shelly showed up and announced to everyone that breakfast was ready. Elle and I jumped up, excited by the hopes of coffee, no matter how bad it was, and whatever they might offer. We had survived for days at a time on nothing more than granola bars, dry cereal, and corn chips, with only sips of rationed water. It did not matter what they had prepared, we were grateful. The others had already fallen into a rut. They weighed the value of a less than perfect breakfast against the time they had left, which for some was not long at all. I wanted to stand up on a tabletop in the dining area and shout to them, 'Every single second is precious! Make the most of each one and appreciate every single thing you have, or are given.' My words may have been heard and valued by some while others might only roll their eyes.

We sat down by ourselves and saw Daniel across the room at a table of other young people. His miraculous recovery was inspirational and gave them an inkling of hope. The dining area was more crowded than I had expected. There were more people in the hospital than Elle and I had realized. In all, I had estimated over a hundred people, mostly patients, but nearly twenty of them were staff members and doctors. Conversations were loud and the room was abuzz when we walked in with our small group, but by the time we had taken our seats it had quieted to a hushed murmur. Sideways glances and whispered conversations were directed at Elle and I. We were strangers and outsiders, posing a threat to those who did not understand our plight. In some of their eyes, we were no better than vagrants, wanting to eat their food, take what we can get and move on. I had to question what our real motive was... perhaps on some level they were right. That thought made me nearly lose my appetite until four staff members wheeled out baker's carts with racks of trays, filled with plates and cups, steaming with aromatic fragrances of coffee, bacon, and pancakes.

"What are we celebrating here?" One of the older gentlemen, dressed in a robe and long pajamas, said in a condescending tone. "Is this for the weirdos you let in? Why don't we eat like this every day?" His questions were cruel and hurtful, and they were met with a ruckus of muttered discussion and agreement.

"Quiet down George." Dr. Green stood on a chair, surrounded by his colleagues and staff. "These *weirdos*, as you labeled them, just might be your salvation." The room went silent. "Many of you remember Daniel. Daniel had a malignant tumor that had metastasized to his brain and had gone home to be with his family and friends... yet there he sits; head full of blonde hair, stronger than I've ever seen him, and having no signs or symptoms of cancer. I believe we might be able to reverse the cancerous cells in all of you... if you are willing." The silence was broken by the sound of plates, cups, and silverware meeting the laminate tabletops.

"I'd rather die than be one of them alien things." George stood up, shaking his arthritis riddled fist in the air. He was possibly the oldest, and definitely the most vocal of the bunch.

"And that is your choice and God-given right." A woman from the other side of the room spoke up. "Some of us might want to hear what he has to say. How long did we fight for the right to use cannabis extracts to help fight cancer, and how many people died before they finally agreed to let us? Well, we are on our own now, and they can't tell us what we can and can't do anymore. So sit down and be quiet so the rest of us can listen." George swatted his hand in her direction as if to dismiss what she had said, but the roaring chuckles from the assemblage had him in his seat, post haste.

"You are exactly right... Kassy?" The doctor was hesitant, but the woman nodded, reassuring him that he had her name correct. "No one has to choose this. I am not even sure if it will work, but from what I have seen and the story I was told, this has worked before in the most rudimentary of settings with no real medical professionals involved."

"If you aren't sure if it'll even work, then what exactly are you proposing?" The valid question came from a man, no older than 40, who sat at the table with Kassy. His concern was met with the bobbing heads of many unsure survivors.

"What I propose is that anyone interested in this, we'll call it a project, can sign a waiver of participation and the staff and I will sift through everyone who signs up and make an order of urgency, worst case first and so on. I am going to propose that we begin with one participant at a time and every few days or week if there are no adverse reactions, we will move on to the next." Dr. Green had thought it through and had not even slept since our arrival. "I am sure Daniel and our new friends Mr. Tanner and Elle would be more than happy to tell you everything they know about the process."

"What all is it gonna take to do... whatever we have to do?" Asked a young girl of no more than nine years old, who was sitting with Daniel's group and wearing a knit cap to cover her balding head. The children and young adults that sat together at a group of tables began chattering amongst themselves for a minute and just as Dr. Green was getting down from his chair, Daniel spoke up.

"We all think this is going to be something important... something people will talk about for a long time, we hope." He looked directly at me. "Tell them about the holiday you made up."

I was a little embarrassed but I stood up in front of the crowded room and spoke. "Before Elle and I found Daniel, we were staying with a handful of survivors in a small town called Barnhill. There was an accident and we tried doing what Dr. Green is suggesting as a last resort to save the life of a child... a young girl named Maddie. Long story-short, it was an amazing success and we celebrated with a huge feast shortly after she had fully recovered. Since it was like a new beginning for her and in some respects it was a new beginning for the Barnhill tribe." I shook my head at the words I had chosen. "We called ourselves a tribe. I guess it made us feel like we weren't alone... that somewhere out there, there were other tribes of survivors. Anyway, I've gotten off track. We decided to call our new holiday The Genesis Feast, or Genesis Day." I raised my hand to Daniel, giving the floor back to him and taking my seat again.

"Cool." One of the teens said.

"Yeah, it is." Daniel continued. "Well, what I guess I'm getting at, is that we all think we should have a special name for what we are about to do, for Dr. Green's project and I think it's fitting if we stick with the same theme. Can we call it *The Genesis Project*?" The surrounding tables and even many of the older people cheered at the idea, which caused a huge grin to grow across Daniel's face and the face of many of the young people who had come up with the idea.

"To answer Alyssa's question, it's going to be as simple as getting a small injection on day one, and then later that day, or the following day, having a very small amount of blood drawn to be tested. Those tests may have to be done once a day, or maybe a couple of times a week until we begin to see how the results come out." Dr. Green's explanation was met with gasps of those who were hesitant, but now amazed at the simplicity of it all. "Secondly, I think the idea of a new holiday marking the rebirth of mankind as Genesis Day was a brilliant idea and I think we should all take note of the date and begin to honor it every year on its anniversary. Having my experimental project named is an honor and I cannot think of a more fitting name than *THE GENESIS PROJECT!*" He shouted the last three words and once again it drew cheers and applause from the crowd.

"Where do we sign up?" Alyssa shouted above the roaring din, tossing her cap into the air.

"I'll get the consent waiver written up this morning and if we can get through the signing early enough, we can announce our first candidate in the morning and maybe even administer the first injection in the next few days. I still need to confer with a few of my colleagues and double check the samples we already have." Dr. Green knew that there would not be any snooty lawyer types dissecting it for legalities or loopholes for lawsuits.

"Alright, alright... everyone calm down. Why don't you all enjoy your breakfasts before they get ice cold." Nurse Shelly yelled to the crowd. Everyone sat down and the conversations continued on in a lower volume. "Now... with a show of hands, does anyone want a cup of coffee?"

The crowd went silent and every hand in the room, including George and Alyssa's, shot straight up in the air. "What?" George snarled at the turned heads. "Just 'cause I ain't gonna be no alien, don't mean I don't want coffee. It *is* a human thing you know?"

Nurse Shelly held back a chuckle and called over her shoulder to the restaurant kitchen. "Better put on some more coffee."

Dr. Green and a couple of his associates disappeared while the rest of us began to devour the breakfast feast that had been prepared for us. When one of the staff brought around the carafe of coffee I quizzed her about how they were able to cook a hot breakfast and make coffee. My first thought was that they were running one of the portable generators, but I had not heard the loud grumbling of a gas motor. I was informed that they still had natural gas, which some of the ovens, stovetops, and water heaters ran on. Did I hear right? Hot water? First bacon and coffee and now... hot water. I may never want to leave this place!

As much as I enjoyed the creature comforts of this place and being around so many people, I knew that staying was not really an option. I wasn't sure how soon we could leave, but I knew in my heart that we would have to go long before we really wanted to. Most of our day was spent in the dining room where we had a constant flow of people, usually two or three at a time but sometimes as many as ten, coming to ask questions about our experiences and the changes that had occurred. There were few details we could give them about what they would experience and some of that was only hypothetical. Maddie was the only one who had experienced a trial of what the doctor was suggesting and we had only spent a short time with her after her recovery. She had been given the cat-like night vision and the ability to heal quickly, but whether or not her unpredictable fever spikes were a side effect of the injection or from her deadly infection, we could not say. We could only inform that it could be a possibility. By dusk, we were informed that of the eighty-seven patients, fifty-two had signed and if the first recipient had success, more would likely agree.

The next few days and nights passed slowly, but at least, there were no more nightmares and I found myself feeling rested and recharged. Some of my time were spent searching deep in my thoughts to try to find the place where the information from the Titan had been stored, but I could not locate it. No logical reason existed, but I knew that there was a useful library hidden somewhere within me. Other times we relaxed in the comforts we were offered. Elle and I enjoyed fairly regular meals, warm baths, shaving and clean, though hand washed, clothing. I found myself at the window wall often, looking out in expectation of the return of the Takers and Titans. It was while I stood there looking out at the skyline that I saw a distant steeple and I had an eerie feeling of deja vu.

Chapter 12
Winter

In all, it took the doctors three additional days to deliberate and decide exactly how to move forward with the first trial of The Genesis Project. They had sorted and prioritized the pages of names. The word was spread that there would be an announcement during dinner on the fourth evening but the rumors had already begun to circulate. Elle had heard that the whole project was shut down indefinitely and I had overheard a conversation between a group of the younger volunteers. They were gossiping that Daniel was going to get to pick which one of his friends got treated first, and one of the teens said they heard he would even get to pick who was treated at all. Someone, possibly George, had said that it was a plan by the aliens to take us over; that our trio had been sent by the invaders to infiltrate the hospital and gather up the remaining *humans* and infect them, turning them into alien slaves, like the Takers. The medical professionals had to weigh out the possibility of every rumor and concern, regardless of how improbable.

Day 4: Once again, that morning we were swamped with questions and unlike before, this battery of quizzes felt more like an interrogation. Breakfast consisted of a slice of ham on dry, slightly stale bread. I ate it graciously but wished that it could have been toasted. The one saving grace that came with the *day-old sandwiches* was the first coffee since the Genesis Project announcement. Elle, Daniel and I found we were defending ourselves more often than we were answering genuine questions about the project. More than once I saw Elle giving Daniel's shoulder a comforting squeeze and more than once when intimidating adults made hurtful accusations, Daniel held back his tears and emotions, proving he was more mature than the frightened adults that were two, three or more times his own age.

When lunchtime rolled around, we had become like a drop of oil in a sea of water. We did not mix and felt a separation that was out of our control. There was a surrounding ring of empty tables and leprosy could not have made us feel more like outcasts. Our table was uncomfortably quiet and even Elle and I rarely spoke to each other during the lunch assembly. Daniel sat with us for a short time, but even he did not really speak. Half way through his sandwich Daniel took his meal with him and began to make his rounds, visiting the other tables. I had to give him credit for his bravery and tenacity. The first few tables were cold and unwelcoming, but he did not waver and rooted his way in and began actually sitting with them. He was shattering the icy borders with his boyish charm and familiar face. The team of doctors and staff entered and a hush came over the room.

"You sure you are willing to be our pin cushion for the project?" One of the doctors, Dr. Patel, joked. "Right now, you are the only source of blood donation and we can't store any without refrigeration. Every injection we give would mean a new blood draw from you... or we could just put a port in and open the spigot when needed."

"Whatever it takes to help people... that's what I'm willing to do." Dr. Patel reached out to shake my hand when I reiterated my commitment to the project and the people.

"Can I have everyone's attention, please." Dr. Patel alerted the room and turned the floor over to the Chief Medical Officer on staff, Dr. Green.

"Thank you, Dr. Patel." Dr. Green began. "As many of you have heard through unsubstantiated rumors, we have deliberated and agreed to move ahead with the first test subject of the Genesis Project. We had planned to announce the name this evening and begin in the morning, but we have moved our schedule up and hope to administer the first injection tonight. Joshua Hardin will be the first recipient from the Triple C Tribe." He leaned over and whispered to me. "I hope it's okay that I borrowed the idea of naming our *tribe*. I thought it might make them all feel like they are a part of something."

"We don't have a copyright on naming a tribe, so it's perfectly fine. I'm actually flattered." Elle squeezed my hand, feeling a change in the tides.

The crowd talked amongst themselves, nodding and pointing towards Joshua in a positive way. Joshua said nothing. It must have come as a shock to him that by being named as the first participant, it not only meant there was no success story other than one that was only true to them if they chose to believe it, it also meant that out of the multitude of

169

volunteers, his was the worst case. That made him both frightened to death and thrilled to possibly have a cure that would end the horrible side effects of having chemotherapy. His friends that sat with him patted him on the back and congratulated him. Daniel was one of those friends and Joshua spoke softly into his ear. Daniel took hold of Joshua's wheelchair and rolled him up to Dr. Green and then turned him to face the massive group.

"I just wanted to say..." His voice was weak and everyone fell silent, straining to hear his words. "If it weren't for these *outsiders*, as I've heard some of you call them, I wouldn't be here to see the spring, maybe not even the new year. I know there are no guarantees. It may not help me live any longer. I suppose it might even go the other way... anything could happen. Maybe I'll grow antennas and a third eye." Everyone chuckled through tears and overpowering emotions. "But I am thirty-six years old. That's a short life to some, but it has been filled with some amazing people and experiences." He swallowed hard and asked for a drink of water. "And if this is my last experience... I am honored and thrilled to be a part of something this monumental. If this gives me nothing more than the experience, I am indebted to Dr. Green and these fine people for that experience, and for giving me something I haven't had in a very long time... Hope." Joshua turned to Daniel. "That's it... you can take me back to the table now."

"We are humbled and blessed to be able to offer some hope." Elle stood up as she spoke. "Though you were right... there is no guarantee, but hope truly is far more valuable. If we have given any of you hope, I pray that it is not in vain. Mother Earth and all of the heavens above us have brought us together in this place for a reason. Whatever that reason is, let us make the very best of every moment we have together."

Old man George stood up and I prepared to shut down his derogatory remarks. Instead, he said nothing. He stood there under the scrutinizing eyes of his peers and raised his shaking hands in front of him.

One slow and echoing clap rang out, followed by another and another. One by one, those surrounding him first, stood with him and began to applaud, until the entire room was on their feet if they could stand. There was not a dry eye in the house. Even George and Dr. Patel were misty-eyed and applauding.

Joshua had plenty of support for the rest of the afternoon. Daniel and he became inseparable, but many others, including doctors, nurses and others on the list, surrounded him like he had become a local celebrity. Joshua enjoyed the attention that he was not used to getting, but it was also exhausting. On his way back to the fourth floor, there was no 'bump-bump-bump' up the stairs backwards, being pulled by a struggling nurse. Instead, numerous nurses and orderlies surrounded his chair and smoothly carried him, like an ancient emperor being paraded past his loyal subjects and peasants. There were not as many preparations as there would have been in a fully functional treatment center, but Joshua was offered a nice hot bath and a brand new set of men's long pajamas from the gift shop were opened up for him to wear after he finished bathing. He felt refreshed though still exhausted by all of the attention and activity of the day.

When the sun began to fall lower in the western sky, and the city around us was doused in shadows and a golden glow, a small offering of dinner was brought around to everyone. Mostly it was a choice of water or soda and a variety of prepackaged snacks that would have ended up in a vending machine. A can of Coca-Cola and a small bag of snack mix was my dinner though my stomach was in knots and it was nearly impossible to eat. Maddie and Joshua's situations were similar but different. When we decided to inject Maddie with my blood, we knew she would most likely never make it to the morning. Joshua had only been given months to live, but if something went wrong, if his body rejected the change, he could lose the last few, precious months of his young life. I was torn and distraught by what was the right thing to do. It really did not matter at this point. I had given my word; I had given hope, and I could not back out now.

"We're ready for you now." The familiar smile of Nurse Shelly comforted my nervousness. "Are you ready?"

"I don't know if I'm really ready, but I don't think another few minutes or even hours is going to change that." I stood up to follow her and Elle stood with me. We walked the corridor hand in hand like we were walking the last mile of a death row inmate.

"You're going to be fine." Elle leaned her head against my shoulder as we walked. "You've handled much more difficult things than this."

"Yeah... but I'm not really worried about me." Elle already knew this, but I felt the need to say it aloud anyway.

The trip seemed never ending, but when my nerves had finally started to calm, Nurse Shelly broke the silence again. "Here we are... Right in here."

She pushed open the door and held it for us. It was not a patient room or an operating room but appeared more like a hotel room. It was like walking through a portal from one location to a completely different one. There were two full sized beds with a nightstand in between. The nightstand had been cleared of whatever may have once sat on it and now held a familiar, sturdy, blue, cotton linen covered instrument tray. On the wall opposite was a small entertainment cabinet complete with microwave, refrigerator, and television (if only there were electricity). In one corner, by the window was a cushioned easy chair and on the other side of the window was a dinette with two chairs. Joshua had been helped into the bed farthest from the door. He looked comfortable and ready to begin. A teary-eyed woman had pulled one of the dinette chairs next to the bed and held his hand.

172

"Tanner, Elle..." Joshua's voice was even weaker than before. "This is my fiancé, Amber."

"It's a pleasure to meet you." I started to reach my hand out but quickly realized that she had no intention of letting go of Joshua's hand shake mine, not even for a moment. Instead, she smiled through her tears and nodded in recognition.

"We thought it might be easier if you would lay here." Nurse Shelly motioned to the empty bed. "Not that you need to lie down, but it will make it easier for us to draw the blood and to quickly transfer it to Josh."

"This is quite a setup you have here," I said looking around the room as I sat on the edge of the mattress.

"This room is set aside for family members of terminal patients when their time is very near and they cannot travel home for hospice. It is a courtesy of the Center and our hope is to allow the family to spend as much time as possible with their loved ones, and be near when that time comes."

The heaviness of the surrounding reality settled on my shoulders and I hoped that Joshua's fiancé would not have to experience such a thing. Elle rubbed the tension from my shoulders while I watched Joshua and Amber staring into each other's eyes and whispering amongst themselves. Dr. Green pushed through the door, followed by Dr. Patel.

"I will be here to observe and take notations of the procedure, actions, and reactions that occur." Dr. Patel spoke softly and clearly with his heavy eastern accent. "If everyone could please clear the area between the beds for Dr. Green to perform the procedure."

Amber sat on the far side of Joshua's bed and Elle drug a chair to the far side of mine, leaving the space between open. Nurse Shelly had brought in one of those chrome legged, black leather seated, doctor stools into the room and wheeled it between our beds for Dr. Green to use. He sat on it in front of the nightstand and uncovered the unimpressive array of instruments and medical sundries. Soon the entire room smelled of alcohol swabs and my inner elbow was chilled from the evaporating disinfectant. The Chloraprep had turned our inner elbows a putrid yellow color to avoid contamination, but to me, it seemed a bit over cautious... I was not going to be *infected* by Joshua's cancer, and he was about to be injected with my blood. Whatever had survived the thorough alcohol dousing and scrubbing was not likely to be affected by the yellow prep solution. Either way, it did not matter. The preparations had been done. The syringe had been assembled and we were down to the tourniquet and the stick and burn of the needle.

In mere minutes, the entire procedure was over and we were relaxing with a magical, sparkling unicorn bandage on our arms. I was informed that the bandages were requested by Alyssa and her friend Tabitha. Both were fanatics about unicorns and anything that sparkled. The two girls had sworn that the sparkling unicorns were magical and would make the procedure a success. The nurses and doctors discussed the potential magic of the bandages and believed that mystical properties aside, it would at the very least raise a smile from Joshua and me. When everything was said and done, I was asked to stay for a few hours until Joshua had dozed off to sleep. Amber and Elle stayed with us and one candle-toting staff member was always in and out of the room to check on Joshua. It is a wonder that he was able to even fall sleep.

When the time came, Elle and I retreated to our luxurious penthouse for a few hours of shut-eye. The morning sun came early, shouting our names and blinding us with all of its fiery glory.

"Wake up!" Elle shoved me hard.

"I'm up... I'm up," I grunted at her though I was barely awake.

"Come on. Let's go see how Josh did last night." Her urgency jolted me wide awake.

"Right!" I jumped up and rushed out of the door wearing nothing but my basketball shorts.

"You really going out wearing that?" Elle laughed but got no reply. "Hey! ...wait up!"

Elle hopped into the hall tugging her jeans up over her perfect butt. Her bare feet made an echoed smacking sound on the concrete steps as she descended them, halfheartedly trying to tuck her tank top into her snug fitting pants. She caught up to me just as I opened the door on the third floor where the hotel style, procedure room had been set up. The entire floor was suspiciously quiet and the two of us nervously scurried down the hall to find the room devoid of life... not that Joshua was dead, necessarily, just absent from the room, along with everyone else. Our concern was exponentially heightened when Elle pointed a shaky finger to the window where Joshua's wheelchair sat empty.

"Come on." I grabbed her by the arm. "We've gotta find Dr. Green."

We zipped back down the hall and into the stairs, expecting to find answers on the fifth floor. When we had almost reached the fourth floor, a commotion came from below.

"Hey! Who's there?" A voice we recognized, but couldn't place called up to us.

"Tanner..." I answered back. "... and Elle."

"Down here. Dr. Green and Patel are looking for you in the dining hall." I finally recognized the voice as that of the petite nurse who had shown us to our room on our first night with the *Triple-C tribe*. The name had a ring to it and though it sounded more like a high school gaming group, this group of people had already branded an indelible memory in my mind. We reversed our climb and skipping steps, swiftly hit the second-floor landing. I feared that if both doctors were inquiring of our whereabouts, it might not be good.

The tiny nurse in blue scrubs led the way and a loud clamor of voices came from the dining area. A thought passed through my head that we may be on our way to our own lynching.

"Elle! Tanner! So glad you're here. Someone's been looking for you." Nurse Shelly waved from the front of the dining room.

She stepped aside, and a sight we were not prepared for was revealed. There in the midst of a crowd of early risers stood Joshua with a smile on his face, a brilliant sparkling glow in his eyes and his fiance Amber by his side. Yes... Joshua stood. Something he had not been strong enough to do for even the shortest period of time since before our arrival.

"Here they are!" Dr. Patel actually shouted the opening remarks of a very welcoming speech. "And we must thank Daniel too, for bringing them here. Thanks to the serendipitous event that brought everyone together here. This project is still in its infancy, but it already appears to be the most aggressive and least invasive therapy we have ever seen."

"Enough of the medical mumbo-jumbo..." Dr. Green broke into Patel's speech. "The important thing, I think, is that even if Joshua's days have not been increased, a fact we have no way of knowing for certain, his quality of life has dramatically improved overnight." And with those words a rousing cheer and applause ensued.

***

Over the course of the day, we were thanked by many, hugged by some and wept on by Amber with tears of joy and appreciation. Joshua grew stronger and healthier by the hour and two days passed before they announced that Alyssa would be the next recipient. We grew comfortable with our surroundings and our acquaintances became friends. The time between volunteers shortened as our time there grew longer. Days turned into weeks and the weeks turned to a month. On Christmas Eve, we celebrated with a feast, Christmas carols and two partial bottles of scotch and a full fifth of single malt whiskey. It was a joyous time for everyone there including the nearly dozen Genesis Project volunteers who had or were having amazing recoveries.

According to the staff and doctors, it was the coldest winter in decades. Frost covered windows, and snowflakes on Christmas Eve were not exactly what I had expected to be labeled as *coldest winter in decades*, but it was growing colder inside and the patient and staff areas were shrinking. By Christmas Day, beds, sofas, and every single person were moved to the second floor to share heat generated by cooking once a day and body heat in general. It was cozy with everyone together during every daylight hour and even though the average room temperature had dropped below 60 degrees Fahrenheit, the morale was good. As true as that was, most of the winter was ahead of us and it could prove to be a long, dark and cold time for all of us at the California Cancer Center.

***

It was on the eve of New Year's Eve that our situation at the center dramatically changed. The common room, as we had begun to call the dining room now that we all were on the same floor, was filled. Two dozen tea-light candles adorned the tables and each was crowded with friends. Some of those who had been treated read outdated magazines or books in the dim light and others played cards while most just talked about what they were going to do when they recovered and the weather warmed up. Conversations buzzed with talks of walking or jogging, boating and bicycling. Elle and I sat alone on a small sofa, curled up in each other's arms and basked in the warmth of acceptance. Her baby bump had grown into much more than that. We were feeling almost normal when Daniel sprinted into the room and called out for Dr. Green.

"What's wrong Big D?" I asked, jumping to my feet.

"Where's the doc? It's George. I heard him from down the hall and went to see what was wrong. He didn't look good at all and asked for the doctor. He asked for you too Mr. Tanner." Daniel was obviously shaken up and Nurse Shelly and Alyssa rushed up to calm him.

"What's going on?" Dr. Green came out of the shadows.

"George... something's wrong with George," Elle said, struggling with her big belly as she stood.

Elle, Dr. Green, Daniel, Alyssa and I headed down to George's room. Nurse Shelly grabbed Margybeth, an elderly woman who was one of George's only close friends at the center and followed close behind though Margybeth moved a little slower than we had. Dr. Green had his LED light sticking out of his lab coat pocket and flipped the switch to 'on' as we traveled down the dark and shadowy hallway. We slowed our pace to let the doctor enter the room first and the rest of us surrounded George as he lay still in his bed, only moving his watery eyes to acknowledge our arrival.

"George, can you tell me what's wrong?" Dr. Green asked the clinical question though the inflection in his wavering voice revealed more emotion than he wanted it to.

"Sure I can... I'm dyin', doc." His voice was shallow, but his point was made bluntly... just like George. "I just wanted to tell ya thanks for everything."

"We could fast track you to the front of the line for the Genesis Project if you'd like." The doctor was not ready to lose a patient after having seen so many incredible recoveries.

"Tanner..." George faintly moved his fingers in an attempt to call me over. "I was wrong about you." His eyes wandered to Elle and Daniel for a moment. "I was wrong about all of you. Margybeth, you get on that list tonight. Don't be a hardheaded fool like me." His eyes welled up and the tears rolled down his thin and brittle skin from the outside corners of his sunken eyes and into his thin silver hair.

"It's okay George." I placed my hand on his shoulder. "You are who you are. You held your ground and kept to your convictions, even if it didn't always make everyone your friend, and *that* is a desirable and hard to find quality, my friend. I am a better man for knowing you, but like the doc said, we can do this right here in a matter of minutes. Calling it the *Genesis Project* sounds fancy, but really, it's just an injection." I wiped my watery eyes and Elle stepped up beside me, wrapping her arms around my waist.

"No, it's not okay." George struggled to get his words out. "We've been in the same building for over a month and I don't even know you. I missed out on a chance to know two amazing people." He drew a rattled breath. "Danny... I kinda knew, as well as I knew any of the others, but you two... I avoided and that was a foolish thing."

"George." Elle sniffled back her snotty tears. "You are genuine, and I'm afraid we are the ones who are foolish for not getting to know you."

"Earthchild..." George's eyes glazed over as he reached out to touch Elle's protruding belly. "You are the future... I am the past." His arm was weak and faded back to his side. "I pray that your generation will see the earth and all those who walk beneath the sun as equals... as brothers and sisters."

"That was beautiful George." Margybeth wept openly.

179

"Rubbish..." He jeered and went into a brief coughing fit, unable to catch his breath. Everyone rushed to the edge of his bed though there was nothing anyone could do to help him. "Are you here Margybeth?"

"Yes, I'm here George." She knew he was losing cognition and her heart was breaking.

"I've grown old, very old Margy." He wheezed. "You get on that list and feel better while you can. The Earth has grown tired of me and it is time for me to go." His lips quivered and he fought to draw in one last breath, and with it, he spoke his last words. "Remember me."

George's body relaxed and let go of its last rattling breath. We had lost one person that we could have saved and his passing was both sorrowful and beautiful. In his last moments, he came to know the error of his ways and I wanted nothing more than to believe that those last moments might bring him eternal peace. I held Elle so close and hugged her so tightly, hoping that perhaps our breaking hearts would somehow stay together and remain unbroken.

We hovered around George's bed, awkwardly unsure of how to walk away. I suppose that was the lesson I have learned more than anything from my short friendship with George. We, as a race, find it so easy to walk away from those we love over the tiniest of disagreements and for the most ridiculous reasons. Ironically and inevitably, the time will come that we cannot say good-bye before leaving. The one thing I've learned... Never walk away quickly, as if it were an easy thing to do, for one day it will not be.

The Convergence Saga begins with The Pale Titan by Rick Kueber. Book One

The Pale Titan Complete Book

The Pale Titan Pt. 1   The Pale Titan Pt. 2   The Pale Titan Pt. 3

Stellium Books is releasing this epic Sci-Fi adventure as a serial with a new part coming out each month. The Pale Titan Part 1 released in November 2015.

Follow Rick Kueber's author page here.

Best Sellers in Supernatural

Frost and Flame Trilogy by Rick Kueber

Forever Ash: The Witch Child of Helmach Creek
Shadows of Eternity: The Children of the Owls
Neverending Maddness: A Girl Lost to the World

More Books by Rick Kueber

Amazing Paranormal Encounters Volume 1

Amazon top 10 Best Seller in Supernatural for over 5 months...

Featuring Rick Kueber

Amazing Paranormal Encounters Volume 1

Stellium Books August 2015

Amazing Paranormal Encounters Volume 2

Stellium Books

Amazing Paranormal Encounters Volume 2

Stellium Books February 2016